Thurber on Crime

Thurber on Crime

James Thurber

Edited by Robert Lopresti

HAMISH HAMILTON · LONDON

HAMISH HAMILTON LTD

Published by the Penguin Group
Penguin Books Ltd, 27 Wrights Lane, London w8 5tz, England
Penguin Books USA Inc., 375 Hudson Street, New York, New York 10014, USA
Penguin Books Australia Ltd, Ringwood, Victoria, Australia
Penguin Books Canada Ltd, 10 Alcorn Avenue, Toronto, Ontario, Canada m4v 3b2
Penguin Books (NZ) Ltd, 182–190 Wairau Road, Auckland 10, New Zealand

Penguin Books Ltd, Registered Offices: Harmondsworth, Middlesex, England

First published in the United States of America by Mysterious Press, Warner Books, Inc. 1991
First published in Great Britain by Hamish Hamilton Ltd 1992

10 9 8 7 6 5 4 3 2 1

Copyright © Rosemary A. Thurber, 1991
Foreword copyright © Donald E. Westlake, 1991
Introduction copyright © Robert Lopresti, 1991

Printed in Great Britain by Clays Ltd, St Ives plc

A CIP catalogue record for this book is available from the British Library

ISBN 0-241-13292-4

Contents

Foreword

GENTLE COMEDY is the hardest to make work. The fellow who slips on the banana peel, catches the cream pie smack in the kisser, gets his necktie set on fire—all of those are guaranteed yocks. To laugh at the cartoon character who has already taken three steps into midair before noticing he's gone beyond land's edge, and who has now just time to give us one unbelieving look before the plummet; easy as falling off a cliff. But gentle comedy, comedy in which the disaster is either subtly referential or nonexistent, that's tough. What's funny about a guy who *doesn't* spill the soup in his lap?

In the early days of *The New Yorker*, before that magazine settled into its middle-aged task of being our premier viewer with alarm, it had a much deeper commitment to verbal humor (happily, it retains its commitment to visual humor), and among the slash-and-burn practitioners led by S. J. Perelman (who never saw a window he didn't want to throw a rock through), there were two fellows who time after time made you laugh without having to staunch anybody's wounds later. They were Robert Benchley and James Thurber, and between them they taught me, at the impressionable age at which I first came across them, that it was possible to get where you wanted to go in comedy without running anybody down.

Whatever it was that Robert Benchley did, nobody before or since ever did it so well; or possibly at all. *Sui generis*, he stood, or slumped, alone. On the other hand, he was a very specific kind of miniaturist. Whatever it was he did—and even while reading him, and enjoying him, you could rarely entirely figure out what he was doing—it was what he did every single time. He had dug himself a narrow literary trench, gracefully curved, and he marched in that trench his whole life long.

Thurber was something else. He wrote short stories, he wrote for the Broadway theater, he wrote oddball little fairy tales with even odder morals attached, he wrote reportage, he wrote articles on all kinds of subjects both comic and serious, he wrote parodies, he even occasionally wrote things kind of like whatever it was Robert Benchley was doing. ("How the Kooks Crumble," in the present collection, in which the writer keeps forgetting he's here to complain about radio, shows some of that quality, here and there . . . in part.) And when he paused in all that writing, Thurber drew cartoons.

About those cartoons. When someone once criticized Harold Ross, *The New Yorker*'s first editor, for keeping on the staff "a fifth-rate artist like Thurber," Ross replied, "You're wrong, Thurber is a third-rate artist." I don't know about that; Ross was a kindly man. In fact, anybody who can't draw better than James Thurber probably has trouble tying his own shoelaces.

But so what? Cartoons are not about their form, they're about their substance. The wonderful weirdness of Thurber's mind is probably best apprehended in these agonizingly amateurish little squiggles. With no technique and hardly any skill, Thurber nevertheless managed to communicate an entire skewed world view with just a few lines on paper. (My own favorite in the present collection is the one with the kangaroo; I never see it without laughing all over again, surprised all over again.)

It had never occurred to me, before *Thurber on Crime* dropped on my head, how often the skewed Thurber view of the world and all its works contained some element of the criminous. After all, if gentle comedy is hard, gentle crime must be even harder. But Thurber makes it look easy.

For instance. We have in these pages a story concerning a rather clever scheme for a perfect murder, in which the murder doesn't manage to take place but the scheme works perfectly anyway. And when another Thurber character actually does resort to murder, the reason is so arcane that the police reject it at once: "Take more'n [such a reason] to cause a mess like that," says the trooper at the crime scene.

Thurber's interest in the world of crime seems to have been that of the timid man testing his resolve against his fears. He shows himself capable of straight reportage on the famous Hall-Mills murder case, and again on the strange case of the fellow at *The New Yorker* who'd embezzled from Ross for years without being at all suspected. Or he can turn his attention to a real-life kidnapping with absurd elements and raise that absurdity to hilarious art by telling the story as a Horatio Alger tale; the best Alger parody I've ever read.

Thurber's fictional characters usually live in a fog of bewilderment, but get where they're going anyway. His old friend at *The New Yorker*, Wolcott Gibbs, once said, "Thurber has a firm grasp on confusion," and this confusion may, in fact, be his characters' best defensive weapon; they overcome danger by failing to recognize it, as with the title character in "The Man Who Knew Too Little."

Thurber's interest in crime also led him quite naturally to an interest in, or at least a consideration of, the detective story, and the detective story does not at all emerge unscathed. The woman who reads *Macbeth* as though it were just another traditional detective story does, unfortunately, represent all too well the mindset of the Jessica Fletcher school of crime solving. There are also nice parodies of Cain and spy novels among others, and a surprising little comment about Dashiell Hammett; surprising and, I'm sure, accurate.

Thurber's gentleness and mild air of bewilderment no doubt came at least in part from an accident in his childhood. When he was six, one of his brothers accidentally shot him with an arrow, causing the loss of his left eye. His right eye, never particularly strong, failed when he was forty, and he spent the last quarter century of his life blind.

The blind cartoonist; is that a Thurber joke? Well, Thurber himself once said he planned to title his autobiography *Long Time No See*.

He didn't, in fact. The entire body of his work is his autobiography, really, a solid portion of it collected in this volume. Thurber was Mr. Bruhl and Mr. Preble and all of them. In other precincts, he was Walter Mitty, whose secret life was both a famous short story and a vastly popular movie starring Danny Kaye. And certainly he was *The Male Animal*, a Broadway play, a theater success twice (in 1940 and revived in 1957), as well as one of Henry Fonda's better movies. He is the man whose lifelong love of bloodhounds is herein chronicled, but whose constant drawings of bloodhounds invariably show animals who, while they could surely track you down, would then be too polite to point.

Thurber on crime. There's nothing in the world quite like it.

—Donald E. Westlake

Introduction

I HAVE A CONFESSION to make. I would not want to swear in court that every page of *Thurber on Crime* is about crime.

Most of it is, yes. You will find murder within these pages, both gangland and domestic varieties. You will find smuggling, robbery, kidnapping, and a fine assortment of mayhem.

But is *everything* in here about crime?

Take, for instance, the drawings. In some there are weapons to be seen, or threats in the caption. These are a great comfort to an editor who claims to be producing a book about crime. But what are we to make of the kangaroo in the courtroom? Certainly the man in the witness box is guilty of something; it shows all over his face. But is the kangaroo a victim? An accomplice? A *weapon?*

You'll have to reach your own verdict on that.

Another example would be the set of illustrations Thurber did for "The Raven." Edgar Allan Poe is so thoroughly attached to the history of the detective story that I make no apology for including Thurber's wonderful sketches, even though the poem contains no crime.

(A word of warning to the literary critics who are even now rushing off to write letters explaining that "The Raven" is *really* about murder, or incest, or unpaid parking tickets. Unless your explanation is as funny as Thurber's "Macbeth Murder Mystery," please keep it to yourself.)

To take another example, from the writing this time, "The Casebook of James Thurber" involves no crime, unless you count (as *he* certainly would) the attempted murder of the English language. Thurber certainly saw it as a detective story of sorts, as the title demonstrates, and so it earns a place here. "The Topaz Cufflink Mystery" is included for similar reasons.

In some other stories the crimes apparently take place only in a character's imagination, or even his dreams. (Which reminds me: dueling is illegal now, but was it a crime two hundred years ago? And if a duel takes place half in the twentieth century and half in the nineteenth, where does one file charges?)

The various dogs that appear in his reporting pieces and his fables are all police dogs, whatever breed they happen to be. Thurber's portrayal of these "flatpaws," deserves a place in the annals of crime.

Most of the pieces in this collection are taken from Thurber's books and I have not changed them in any way. The items in "Cuttings" are an exception. Only a small section of these pieces referred to crime, but those sections were too good to miss. In each case I have listed the source so you can see whether I am guilty of violence to the original.

Five of the stories have never, to the best of my knowledge, appeared in any previous Thurber collection. They are "Gang War, 1940," "Izzy and Moe," "The Man Who Knew Too Little," "Little Joe," and "Tom, the Young Kidnapper." Each originally appeared in *The New Yorker*.

"Izzy and Moe" was part of the same "Where Are They Now?" series that provides us with "A Sort of Genius," and "Two O'Clock at the Metropole." I shortened it slightly for this book, removing some details, such as addresses, which seem irrelevent at this late date.

One final note for anyone not familiar with the body of Thurber's work. "The Secret Life of Harold Winney" is nonfiction, a chapter from *The Years With Ross*, Thurber's informal biography of Harold Ross and his magazine, *The New Yorker*. Ross also appears in "Cuttings."

Glancing back to the beginning of this piece I realize that I seem to be apologizing for creating a new collection of Thurber. If so, I apologize for the apology. No excuse is necessary for providing a chance to look at the Master's work in a new context. From the perfect crime of "The Catbird Seat" to the foreign intrigue of "The Lady on 142," Thurber remains as delightfully unexpected as, well, as the kangaroo in the courtroom.

Last but by no means least, it is my pleasure to report that the drawings on pages 147 and 148 are previously unpublished. They are making their first appearance courtesy of Rosemary Thurber, whose permission and cooperation made this project possible.

I rest my case.

—ROBERT LOPRESTI

The Catbird Seat

M R. MARTIN bought the pack of Camels on Monday night in the most crowded cigar store on Broadway. It was theater time and seven or eight men were buying cigarettes. The clerk didn't even glance at Mr. Martin, who put the pack in his overcoat pocket and went out. If any of the staff at F & S had seen him buy the cigarettes, they would have been astonished, for it was generally known that Mr. Martin did not smoke and never had. No one saw him.

It was just a week to the day since Mr. Martin had decided to rub out Mrs. Ulgine Barrows. The term *rub out* pleased him because it suggested nothing more than the correction of an error—in this case an error of Mr. Fitweiler. Mr. Martin had spent each night of the past week working out his plan and examining it. As he walked home now he went over it again. For the hundredth time he resented the element of imprecision, the margin of guesswork that entered into the business. The project as he had worked it out was casual and bold, the risks were considerable. Something might go wrong anywhere along the line. And therein lay the cunning of his scheme. No one would ever see in it the cautious, painstaking hand of Erwin Martin, head of the filing department at F & S, of whom Mr. Fitweiler had once said, "Man is fallible but Martin isn't." No one would see his hand, that is, unless it were caught in the act.

Sitting in his apartment, drinking a glass of milk, Mr. Martin reviewed his case against Mrs. Ulgine Barrows, as he had every night for seven nights. He began at the beginning. Her quacking voice and braying laugh had first profaned the halls of F & S on March 7, 1941 (Mr. Martin had a head for dates). Old Roberts, the personnel chief, had introduced her as the newly appointed special adviser to the president of the firm, Mr. Fitweiler. The woman had appalled Mr. Martin instantly, but he hadn't shown it. He had given her his dry hand, a look of studious concentration, and a faint smile. "Well," she had said, looking at the papers on his desk, "are you lifting the oxcart out of the ditch?" As Mr. Martin recalled that moment, over his milk, he squirmed slightly. He must keep his mind on her crimes as a special adviser, not on her peccadilloes as a personality. This he found difficult to do, in spite of entering an objection and sustaining it. The faults of the woman as a woman kept chattering on in his mind like an unruly witness. She had, for almost two years now, baited him. In the halls, in the elevator, even in his own office, into which she romped now and then like a circus horse, she was constantly shouting these silly questions at him. "Are you lifting the oxcart out of the ditch? Are you tearing up the pea patch? Are you hollering down the rain barrel? Are you scraping around the bottom of the pickle barrel? Are you sitting in the catbird seat?"

It was Joey Hart, one of Mr. Martin's two assistants, who had explained what the gibberish meant. "She must be a Dodger fan," he had said. "Red Barber announces the Dodger games over the radio and he uses those expressions—picked 'em up down South." Joey had gone on to explain one or two. "Tearing up the pea patch" meant going on a rampage; "sitting in the catbird seat" meant sitting pretty, like a batter with three balls and no strikes on him. Mr. Martin dismissed all this with an effort. It had been annoying, it had driven him near to distraction, but he was too solid a man to be moved to murder by anything so childish. It was fortunate, he reflected as he passed on to the important charges against Mrs. Barrows, that he had stood up under it so well. He had maintained always an outward appearance of polite tolerance. "Why, I even believe you like the woman," Miss Paird, his other assistant, had once said to him. He had simply smiled.

A gavel rapped in Mr. Martin's mind and the case proper was resumed. Mrs. Ulgine Barrows stood charged with willful, blatant, and persistent attempts to destroy the efficiency and system of F & S. It was competent, material, and relevant to review her advent and rise to power. Mr. Martin had got the story from Miss Paird, who seemed always able to find things out. According to her, Mrs. Barrows had met Mr. Fitweiler at a party, where she had rescued him from the embraces of a powerfully built drunken man who had mistaken the president of F & S for a famous retired Middle Western football coach. She had led him to a sofa and somehow worked upon him a monstrous magic. The aging gentleman had jumped to the conclusion there and then that this was a woman of singular attainments, equipped to bring out the best in him and in the firm. A week later he had introduced her into F & S as his special adviser. On that day confusion got its foot in the door. After Miss Tyson, Mr. Brundage, and Mr. Bartlett had been fired and Mr. Munson had taken his hat and stalked out, mailing in his resignation later, old Roberts had been emboldened to speak to Mr. Fitweiler. He mentioned that Mr. Munson's department had been "a little disrupted" and hadn't they perhaps better resume the old system there? Mr. Fitweiler had said certainly not. He had the greatest faith in Mrs. Barrow's ideas. "They require a little seasoning, a little seasoning, is all," he had added. Mr. Roberts had given it up. Mr. Martin reviewed in detail all the changes wrought by Mrs. Barrows. She had begun chipping at the cornices of the firm's edifice and now she was swinging at the foundation stones with a pickaxe.

Mr. Martin came now, in his summing up, to the afternoon of Monday, November 2, 1942—just one week ago. On that day, at 3 P.M., Mrs. Barrows had bounced into his office. "Boo!" she had yelled. "Are you scraping around the bottom of the pickle barrel?" Mr. Martin had looked at her from under his green eyeshade, saying nothing. She had begun to wander about the office, taking it in with her great, popping eyes. "Do you really need *all* these filing cabinets?" she had demanded suddenly. Mr. Martin's heart had jumped. "Each of these files," he had said, keeping his voice even, "plays an indispensable part in the system of F & S." She had brayed at him, "Well, don't tear up the pea patch!" and gone to the door. From there she had bawled, "But you sure have got a lot of fine scrap in here!" Mr. Martin could no longer doubt that the finger was on his beloved department. Her pickaxe was on the upswing, poised for the first blow. It had not come yet; he had received no blue memo from the enchanted Mr. Fitweiler bearing nonsensical instructions deriving from the obscene woman. But there was no doubt in Mr. Martin's mind that one would be forthcoming. He must act quickly. Already a precious week had gone by. Mr. Martin stood up in his living room, still holding his milk glass. "Gentlemen of the jury," he said to himself. "I demand the death penalty for this horrible person."

The next day Mr. Martin followed his routine, as usual. He polished his glasses more often and once sharpened an already sharp pencil, but not even Miss Paird noticed. Only once did he catch sight of his victim; she swept past him in the hall with a patronizing "Hi!" At five-thirty he walked home, as usual, and had a glass of milk, as usual. He had never drunk anything stronger in his life—unless you could count ginger ale. The late Sam Schlosser, the S of F & S, had praised Mr. Martin at a staff meeting several years before for his temperate habits. "Our most efficient worker neither drinks nor smokes," he had said. "The results speak for themselves." Mr. Fitweiler had sat by, nodding approval.

Mr. Martin was still thinking about that red-letter day as he walked over to the Schrafft's on Fifth Avenue near Forty-sixth Street. He got there, as he always did, at eight o'clock. He finished his dinner and the financial page of the *Sun* at a quarter to nine, as he always did. It was his custom after dinner to take a walk. This time he walked down Fifth Avenue at a casual pace.

His gloved hands felt moist and warm, his forehead cold. He transferred the Camels from his overcoat to a jacket pocket. He wondered, as he did so, if they did not represent an unnecessary note of strain. Mrs. Barrows smoked only Luckies. It was his idea to puff a few puffs on a Camel (after the rubbing-out), stub it out in the ashtray holding her lipstick-stained Luckies, and thus drag a small red herring across the trail. Perhaps it was not a good idea. It would take time. He might even choke, too loudly.

Mr. Martin had never seen the house on West Twelfth Street where Mrs. Barrows lived, but he had a clear enough picture of it. Fortunately, she had bragged to everybody about her ducky first-floor apartment in the perfectly darling three-storey red-brick. There would be no doorman or other attendants; just the tenants of the second and third floors. As he walked along, Mr. Martin realized that he would get there before nine-thirty. He had considered walking north on Fifth Avenue from Schrafft's to a point from which it would take him until ten o'clock to reach the house. At that hour people were less likely to be coming in or going out. But the procedure would have made an awkward loop in the straight thread of his casualness, and he had abandoned it. It was impossible to figure when people would be entering or leaving the house, anyway. There was a great risk at any hour. If he ran into anybody, he would simply have to place the rubbing-out of Ulgine Barrows in the inactive file forever. The same thing would hold true if there were someone in her apartment. In that case he would just say that he had been passing by, recognized her charming house and thought to drop in.

It was eighteen minutes after nine when Mr. Martin turned into Twelfth Street. A man passed him, and a man and a woman talking. There was no one within fifty paces when he came to the house, halfway down the block. He was up the steps and in the small vestibule in no time, pressing the bell under the card that said "Mrs. Ulgine Barrows." When the clicking in the lock started, he jumped forward against the door. He got inside fast, closing the door behind him. A bulb in a lantern hung from the hall ceiling on a chain seemed to give a monstrously bright light.

There was nobody on the stair, which went up ahead of him along the left wall. A door opened down the hall in the wall on the right. He went toward it swiftly, on tiptoe.

"Well, for God's sake, look who's here!" bawled Mrs. Barrows, and her braying laugh rang out like the report of a shotgun. He rushed past her like a football tackle, bumping her. "Hey, quit shoving!" she said, closing the door behind them. They were in her living room, which seemed to Mr. Martin to be lighted by a hundred lamps. "What's after you?" she said. "You're as jumpy as a goat." He found he was unable to speak. His heart was wheezing in his throat. "I—yes," he finally brought out. She was jabbering and laughing as she started to help him off with his coat. "No, no," he said. "I'll put it here." He took it off and put it on a chair near the door. "Your hat and gloves, too," she said. "You're in a lady's house." He put his hat on top of the coat. Mrs. Barrows seemed larger than he had thought. He kept his gloves on. "I was passing by," he said. "I recognized—is there anyone here?" She laughed louder than ever. "No," she said, "we're all alone. You're as white as a sheet, you funny man. Whatever *has* come over you? I'll mix you a toddy." She started toward a door across the room. "Scotch-and-soda be all right? But say, you don't drink, do you?" She turned and gave him her amused look. Mr. Martin pulled himself together. "Scotch-and-soda will be all right," he heard himself say. He could hear her laughing in the kitchen.

Mr. Martin looked quickly around the living room for the weapon. He had counted on finding one there. There were andirons and a poker and something in a corner that looked like an Indian club. None of them would do. It couldn't be that way. He began to pace around. He came to a desk. On it lay a metal paper knife with an ornate handle. Would it be sharp enough? He reached for it and knocked over a small brass jar. Stamps spilled out of it and it fell to the floor with a clatter. "Hey," Mrs. Barrows yelled from the kitchen, "are you tearing up the pea patch?" Mr. Martin gave a strange laugh. Picking up the knife, he tried its point against his left wrist. It was blunt. It wouldn't do.

* * *

When Mrs. Barrows reappeared, carrying two highballs, Mr. Martin, standing there with his gloves on, became acutely conscious of the fantasy he had wrought. Cigarettes in his pocket, a drink prepared for him—it was all too grossly improbable. It was more than that; it was impossible. Somewhere in the back of his mind a vague idea stirred, sprouted. "For heaven's sake, take off those gloves," said Mrs. Barrows. "I always wear them in the house," said Mr. Martin. The idea began to bloom, strange and wonderful. She put the glasses on a coffee table in front of a sofa and sat on the sofa. "Come over here, you odd little man," she said. Mr. Martin went over and sat beside her. It was difficult getting a cigarette out of the pack of Camels, but he managed it. She held a match for him, laughing. "Well," she said, handing him his drink, "this is perfectly marvelous. You with a drink and a cigarette."

Mr. Martin puffed, not too awkwardly, and took a gulp of the highball. "I drink and smoke all the time," he said. He clinked his glass against hers. "Here's nuts to that old windbag, Fitweiler," he said, and gulped again. The stuff tasted awful, but he made no grimace. "Really, Mr. Martin," she said, her voice and posture changing, "you are insulting our employer." Mrs. Barrows was now all special adviser to the president. "I am preparing a bomb," said Mr. Martin, "which will blow the old goat higher than hell." He had only had a little of the drink, which was not strong. It couldn't be that. "Do you take dope or something?" Mrs. Barrows asked coldly. "Heroin," said Mr. Martin. "I'll be coked to the gills when I bump that old buzzard off." "Mr. Martin!" she shouted, getting to her feet. "That will be all of that. You must go at once." Mr. Martin took another swallow of his drink. He tapped his cigarette out in the ashtray and put the pack of Camels on the coffee table. Then he got up. She stood glaring at him. He walked over and put on his hat and coat. "Not a word about this," he said, and laid an index finger against his lips. All Mrs. Barrows could bring out was "Really!" Mr. Martin put his hand on the doorknob. "I'm sitting in the catbird seat," he said. He stuck his tongue out at her and left. Nobody saw him go.

Mr. Martin got to his apartment, walking, well before eleven. No one saw him go in. He had two glasses of milk after brushing his teeth, and he felt elated. It wasn't tipsiness, because he hadn't been tipsy. Anyway, the walk had worn off all effects of the whisky. He got in bed and read a magazine for a while. He was asleep before midnight.

Mr. Martin got to the office at eight-thirty the next morning, as usual. At a quarter to nine, Ulgine Barrows, who had never before arrived at work before ten, swept into his office. "I'm reporting to Mr. Fitweiler now!" she shouted. "If he turns you over to the police, it's no more than you deserve." Mr. Martin gave her a look of shocked surprise. "I beg your pardon?" he said. Mrs. Barrows snorted and bounced out of the room, leaving Miss Paird and Joey Hart staring after her. "What's the matter with that old devil now?" asked Miss Paird. "I have no idea," said Mr. Martin, resuming his work. The other two looked at him and then at each other. Miss Paird got up and went out. She walked slowly past the closed door of Mr. Fitweiler's office. Mrs. Barrows was yelling inside, but she was not braying. Miss Paird could not hear what the woman was saying. She went back to her desk.

Forty-five minutes later, Mrs. Barrows left the president's office and went into her own, shutting the door. It wasn't until half an hour later that Mr. Fitweiler sent for Mr. Martin. The head of the filing department, neat, quiet, attentive, stood in front of the old man's desk. Mr. Fitweiler was pale and nervous. He took his glasses off and twiddled them. He made a small, bruffing sound in his throat. "Martin," he said, "you have been with us more than twenty years." "Twenty-two, sir," said Mr. Martin. "In that time," pursued the president, "your work and your—uh—manner have been exemplary." "I trust so, sir," said Mr. Martin. "I have understood, Martin," said Mr. Fitweiler, "that you have never taken a drink or smoked." "That is correct, sir," said Mr. Martin. "Ah, yes." Mr. Fitweiler polished his glasses. "You may describe what you did after leaving the office yesterday, Martin," he said. Mr. Martin allowed less than a second for his bewildered pause. "Certainly, sir," he said. "I walked home. Then I went to Schrafft's for dinner. Afterward I walked home again. I went to bed early, sir, and read a magazine for a while. I was asleep before eleven." "Ah, yes," said Mr. Fitweiler again. He was silent for a moment, searching for the proper words to say to the head of the filing department. "Mrs. Barrows," he said finally, "Mrs. Barrows has worked hard, Martin, very hard. It grieves me to report that she has suffered a severe breakdown. It has taken the form of a persecution complex accompanied by distressing hallucinations." "I am very sorry, sir," said Mr. Martin. "Mrs. Barrows is under the delusion," continued Mr. Fitweiler, "that you visited her last evening and behaved yourself in an—uh—unseemly manner." He raised his hand to silence Mr. Martin's little pained outcry. "It is the nature of these psychological diseases," Mr. Fitweiler said, "to fix upon the least likely and most innocent party as the—uh—source of persecution. These matters are not for the lay mind to grasp, Martin. I've just had my psychiatrist, Dr. Fitch, on the phone. He would not, of course, commit himself, but he made enough generalizations to substantiate my suspicions. I suggested to Mrs. Barrows when she had completed her—uh—story to me this morning, that she visit Dr. Fitch, for I suspected a condition at once. She flew, I regret to say, into a rage, and demanded—uh—requested that I call you on the carpet. You may not know, Martin, but Mrs. Barrows had planned a reorganization of your department—subject to my approval, of course, subject to my approval. This brought you, rather than anyone else, to her mind—but again that is a phenomenon for Dr. Fitch and not for us. So, Martin, I am afraid Mrs. Barrows' usefulness here is at an end." "I am dreadfully sorry, sir," said Mr. Martin.

It was at this point that the door to the office blew open with the suddenness of a gas-main explosion and Mrs. Barrows catapulted through it. "Is the little rat denying it?" she screamed. "He can't get away with that!" Mr. Martin got up and moved discreetly to a point beside Mr. Fitweiler's chair. "You drank and smoked at my apartment," she bawled at Mr. Martin, "and you know it! You called Mr. Fitweiler an old windbag and said you were going to blow him up when you got coked to the gills on your heroin!" She stopped yelling to catch her breath and a new glint came into her popping eyes. "If you weren't such a drab, ordinary little man," she said, "I'd think you'd planned it all. Sticking your tongue out, saying you were sitting in the catbird seat, because you thought no one would believe me when I told it! My God, it's really too perfect!" She brayed loudly and hysterically, and the fury was on her again. She glared at Mr. Fitweiler. "Can't you see how he has tricked us, you old fool? Can't you see his little game?" But Mr. Fitweiler had been surreptitiously pressing all the buttons under the top of his desk and employees of F & S began pouring into the room. "Stockton," said Mr. Fitweiler, "you and Fishbein will take Mrs. Barrows to her home. Mrs. Powell, you will go with them." Stockton, who had played a little football in high school, blocked Mrs. Barrows as she made for Mr. Martin. It took him and Fishbein together to force her out of the door into the hall, crowded with stenographers and office boys. She was still screaming imprecations at Mr. Martin, tangled and contradictory imprecations. The hubbub finally died out down the corridor.

"I regret that this has happened," said Mr. Fitweiler. "I shall ask you to dismiss it from your mind, Martin." "Yes, sir," said Mr. Martin, anticipating his chief's "That will be all" by moving to the door. "I will dismiss it." He went out and shut the door, and his step was light and quick in the hall. When he entered his department he had slowed down to his customary gait, and he walked quietly across the room to the W20 file, wearing a look of studious concentration.

A Sort of Genius

O N THE MORNING of Saturday the 16th of September, 1922, a boy named Raymond Schneider and a girl named Pearl Bahmer, walking down a lonely lane on the outskirts of New Brunswick, New Jersey, came upon something that made them rush to the nearest house in Easton Avenue, around the corner, shouting. In that house an excited woman named Grace Edwards listened to them wide-eyed and then telephoned the police. The police came on the run and examined the young people's discovery: the bodies of a man and a woman. They had been shot to death and the woman's throat was cut. Leaning against one of the man's shoes was his calling card, not as if it had fallen there but as if it had been placed there. It bore the name Rev. Edward W. Hall. He had been the rector of the Protestant Episcopal Church of St. John the Evangelist in New Brunswick. The woman was identified as Mrs. Eleanor R. Mills, wife of the sexton of that church. Raymond Schneider and Pearl Bahmer had stumbled upon what was to go down finally in the annals of our crime as perhaps the country's most remarkable mystery. Nobody was ever found guilty of the murders. Before the case was officially closed, a hundred and fifty persons had had their day in court and on the front pages of the newspapers. The names of two must already have sprung to your mind: Mrs. Jane Gibson, called by the avid press "the pig woman," and William Carpender Stevens, once known to a hundred million people simply as "Willie." The pig woman died eleven years ago, but Willie Stevens is alive. He still lives in the house that he lived in fourteen years ago with Mr. and Mrs. Hall, at 23 Nichol Avenue, New Brunswick.

It was from that house that the Rev. Mr. Hall walked at around seven-thirty on the night of Thursday the 14th of September, 1922, to his peculiar doom. With the activities in that house after Mr. Hall's departure the State of New Jersey was to be vitally concerned. No. 23 Nichol Avenue was to share with De Russey's Lane, in which the bodies were found, the morbid interest of a whole nation four years later, when the case was finally brought to trial. What actually happened in De Russey's Lane on the night of September 14th? What actually happened at 23 Nichol Avenue the same night? For the researchers, it is a matter of an involved and voluminous court record, colorful and exciting in places, confused and repetitious in others. Two things, however, stand out as sharply now as they did on the day of their telling: the pig woman's story of the people she saw in De Russey's Lane that night, and Willie Stevens' story of what went on in the house in Nichol Avenue. Willie's story, brought out in cross-examination by a prosecutor whose name you may have forgotten (it was Alexander Simpson), lacked all the gaudy melodrama of the pig woman's tale, but in it, and in the way he told it on the stand, was the real drama of the Hall-Mills trial. When the State failed miserably in its confident purpose of breaking Willie Stevens down, the verdict was already written on the wall. The rest of the trial was anticlimax. The jury that acquitted Willie, and his sister, Mrs. Frances Stevens Hall, and his brother, Henry Stevens, was out only five hours.

A detailed recital of all the fantastic events and circumstances of the Hall-Mills case would fill a large volume. If the story is vague in your mind, it is partly because its edges, even under the harsh glare of investigation, remained curiously obscure and fuzzy. Everyone remembers, of course, that the minister was deeply involved with Mrs. Mills, who sang in his choir; their affair had been for some time the gossip of their circle. He was forty-one, she was in her early thirties; Mrs. Hall was nearing fifty. On the 14th of September, Mr. Hall had dinner at home with his wife, Willie Stevens, and a little niece of Mrs. Hall's. After dinner, he said, according to his wife and his brother-in-law, that he was going to call on Mrs. Mills. There was something about a payment on a doctor's bill. Mrs. Mills had had an operation and the Halls had paid for it (Mrs. Hall had inherited considerable wealth from her parents). He left the house at about the same time, it came out later, that Mrs. Mills left her house, and the two were found murdered, under a crab apple tree in De Russey's Lane, on the edge of town, some forty hours later. Around the bodies were scattered love letters which the choir singer had written to the minister. No weapons were found, but there were several cartridge shells from an automatic pistol.

The investigation that followed—marked, said one New Jersey lawyer, by "bungling stupidity"—resulted in the failure of the grand jury to indict anyone. Willie Stevens was questioned for hours, and so was Mrs. Hall. The pig woman told her extraordinary story of what she saw and heard in the lane that night, but she failed to impress the grand jurors. Four years went by, and the Hall-Mills case was almost forgotten by people outside of New Brunswick when, in a New Jersey court, one Arthur Riehl brought suit against his wife, the former Louise Geist, for annulment of their marriage. Louise Geist had been, at the time of the murders, a maid in the Hall household. Riehl said in the course of his testimony that his wife had told him "she knew all about the case but had been given $5,000 to hold her tongue." This was all that Mr. Philip Payne, managing editor of the *Daily Mirror*, nosing around for a big scandal of some sort, needed. His newspaper "played up" the story until finally, under its goading, Governor Moore of New Jersey appointed Alexander Simpson special prosecutor with orders to reopen the case. Mrs. Hall and Willie Stevens were arrested and so was their brother, Henry Stevens, and a cousin, Henry de la Bruyere Carpender.

At a preliminary hearing in Somerville the pig woman, with eager stridency, told her story again. About nine o'clock on the night of September 14th, she heard a wagon going along Hamilton Road near the farm on which she raised her pigs. Thieves had been stealing her corn and she thought maybe they were at it again. So she saddled her mule, Jenny (soon to become the most famous quadruped in the country), and set off in grotesque pursuit. In the glare of an automobile's headlights in De Russey's Lane, she saw a woman with white hair who was wearing a tan coat, and a man with a heavy moustache, who looked like a colored man. These figures she identified as Mrs. Hall and Willie Stevens. Tying her mule to a cedar tree, she started toward the scene on foot and heard voices raised in quarrel: "Somebody said something about letters." She now saw three persons (later on she increased this to four), and a flashlight held by one of them illuminated the face of a man she identified first as Henry Carpender, later as Henry Stevens, and it "glittered on something" in the man's hand. Suddenly there was a shot, and as she turned and ran for her mule, there were three more shots; a woman's voice screamed, "Oh, my! Oh, my! Oh, my!" and the voice of another woman moaned, "Oh, Henry!" The pig woman rode wildly home on her mule, without investigating further. But she had lost one of her moccasins in her flight, and some three hours later, at one o'clock, she rode her mule back again to see if she could find it. This time, by the light of the moon, she saw Mrs. Hall, she said, kneeling in the lane, weeping. There was no one else there. The pig woman did not see any bodies.

Mrs. Jane Gibson became, because of her remarkable story, the chief witness for the State, as Willie Stevens was to become the chief witness for the defense. If he and his sister were not in De Russey's Lane, as the pig woman had shrilly insisted, it remained for them to tell the detailed story of their whereabouts and their actions that night after Mr. Hall left the house. The grand jury this time indicted all four persons implicated by the pig woman, and the trial began on November 3rd, 1926.

The first persons Alexander Simpson called to the stand were "surprise witnesses." They were a Mr. and Mrs. John S. Dixon, who lived in North Plainfield, New Jersey, about twelve miles from New Brunswick. It soon became apparent that they were to form part of a net that Simpson was preparing to draw around Willie Stevens. They testified that at about eight-thirty on the night of the murders Willie had appeared at their house, wearing a loose-fitting suit, a derby, a wing collar with bow tie, and, across his vest, a heavy gold chain to which was attached a gold watch. He had said that his sister had let him out there from her automobile and that he was trying to find the Parker Home for the Aged, which was at Bound Brook. He stuttered and he told them that he was an epileptic. They directed him to a trolley car and he went stumbling away. When Mrs. Dixon identified Willie as her visitor, she walked over to him and took his right hand and shook it vigorously, as if to wring recognition out of him. Willie stared at her, said nothing. When she returned to the stand, he grinned widely. That was one of many bizarre incidents that marked the progress of the famous murder trial. It deepened the mystery that hung about the strange figure of Willie Stevens. People could hardly wait for him to take the stand.

William Carpender Stevens had sat in court for sixteen days before he was called to the witness chair, on the 23rd of November, 1926. On that day the trial of Albert B. Fall and Edward L. Doheny, defendants in the notorious Teapot Dome scandal, opened in Washington, but the nation had eyes only for a small, crowded courtroom in Somerville, New Jersey. Willie Stevens, after all these weeks, after all these years, was to speak out in public for the first time. As the *New York Times* said, "He had been pictured as 'Crazy Willie,' as a town character, as an oddity, as a butt for all manner of jokes. He had been compared inferentially to an animal, and the hint of an alien racial strain in his parentage had been thrown at him." Moreover, it had been prophesied that Willie would "blow up" on the stand, that he would be trapped into contradictions by the "wily" and "crafty" Alexander Simpson, that he would be tricked finally into blurting out his guilt. No wonder there was no sound in the courtroom except the heavy tread of Willie Stevens' feet as he walked briskly to the witness stand.

Willie Stevens was an ungainly, rather lumpish man, about five feet ten inches tall. Although he looked flabby, this was only because of his loose-fitting clothes and the way he wore them; despite his fifty-four years, he was a man of great physical strength. He had a large head and a face that would be hard to forget. His head was covered with a thatch of thick, bushy hair, and his heavy black eyebrows seemed always to be arched, giving him an expression of perpetual surprise. This expression was strikingly accentuated by large, prominent eyes which, seen through the thick lenses of the spectacles he always wore, seemed to bulge unnaturally. He had a heavy, drooping, walrus moustache, and his complexion was dark. His glare was sudden and fierce; his smile, which came just as quickly, lighted up his whole face and gave him the wide, beaming look of an enormously pleased child. Born in Aiken, South Carolina, Willie Stevens had been brought to New Brunswick when he was two years old. When his wealthy parents died, a comfortable trust fund was left to Willie. The other children, Frances and Henry, had inherited their money directly. Once, when Mrs. Hall was asked if it was not true that Willie was "regarded as essential to be taken care of in certain things," she replied, "In certain aspects." The quality of Willie's mentality, the extent of his eccentricity, were matters the prosecution strove to establish on several occasions. Dr. Laurence Runyon, called by the defense to testify that Willie was not an epileptic and had never stuttered, was cross-examined by Simpson. Said the doctor, "He may not be absolutely normal mentally, but he is able to take care of himself perfectly well. He is brighter than the average person, although he has never advanced as far in school learning as some others. He reads books that are above the average and makes a good many people look like fools." "A sort of genius, in a way, I suppose?" said Simpson. To which the doctor quietly replied, "Yes, that is just what I mean."

There were all sorts of stories about Willie. One of them was that he had once started a fire in his backyard and then, putting on a fireman's helmet, had doused it gleefully with a pail of water. It was known that for years he had spent most of every day at the firehouse of Engine Company No. 3 in Dennis Street, New Brunswick. He played cards with the firemen, ran errands for them, argued and joked with them, and was a general favorite. Sometimes he went out and bought a steak, or a chicken, and it was prepared and eaten in the firehouse by the firemen and Willie. In the days when the engine company had been a volunteer organization, Willie was an honorary member and always carried, in the firemen's parades, a flag he had bought and presented to the firehouse, an elaborate banner costing sixty or seventy dollars. He had also bought the black-and-white bunting with which the front of the firehouse was draped whenever a member of the company died.

After his arrest, he had whiled away the time in his cell reading books on metallurgy. There was a story that when his sister-in-law, Mrs. Henry Stevens, once twitted him on his heavy reading, he said, "Oh, that is merely the bread and butter of my literary repast." The night before the trial opened, Willie's chief concern was about a new blue suit that had been ordered for him and that did not fit him to his satisfaction. He had also lost a collar button, and that worried him; Mrs. Henry Stevens hurried to the jail before the court convened and brought him another one, and he was happy. At the preliminary hearing weeks before, Simpson had declared with brutal directness that Willie Stevens did indeed look like a colored man, as the pig woman had said. At this Willie had half risen from his chair and bared his teeth, as if about to leap on the prosecutor. But he had quickly subsided. Willie Stevens all through the trial had sat quietly, staring. He had been enormously interested when the pig woman, attended by a doctor and a nurse, was brought in on a stretcher to give her testimony. This was the man who now, on trial for his life, climbed into the witness chair in the courtroom at Somerville.

There was an immense stir. Justice Charles W. Parker rapped with his gavel. Mrs. Hall's face was strained and white; this was an ordeal she and her family had been dreading for weeks. Willie's left hand gripped his chair tightly, his right hand held a yellow pencil with which he had fiddled all during the trial. He faced the roomful of eyes tensely. His own lawyer, Senator Clarence E. Case, took the witness first. Willie started badly by understating his age ten years. He said he was forty-four. "Isn't it fifty-four?" asked Case. Willie gave the room his great, beaming smile. "Yes," he chortled, boyishly, as if amused by his slip. The spectators smiled. It didn't take Willie long to dispose of the Dixons, the couple who had sworn he stumbled into their house the night of the murder. He answered half a dozen questions on this point with strong emphasis, speaking slowly and clearly: he had never worn a derby, he had never had epilepsy, he had never stuttered, he had never had a gold watch and chain. Mr. Case held up Willie's old silver watch and chain for the jury to see. When he handed them back, Willie, with fine nonchalance, compared his watch with the clock on the courtroom wall, gave his sister a large, reassuring smile, and turned to his questioner with respectful attention. He described, with technical accuracy, an old revolver of his (the murders had been done with an automatic pistol, not a revolver, but a weapon of the same caliber as Willie's). He said he used to fire off the gun on the Fourth of July; remembering these old holidays, his eyes lighted up with childish glee. From this mood he veered suddenly into indignation and anger. "When was the last time you saw the revolver?" was what set him off. "The last time I saw it was in this courthouse!" Willie almost shouted. "I think it was in October, 1922, when I was taken and put through a very severe grilling by—I cannot mention every person's name, but I remember Mr. Toolan, Mr. Lamb, and Detective David, and they did everything but strike me. They cursed me frightfully." The officers had got him into an automobile "by a subterfuge," he charged. "Mr. David said he simply wanted me to go out in the country, ask me a very few questions, that I would not be very long." It transpired later that on this trip Willie himself had had a question to ask Detective David: would the detective, if they passed De Russey's Lane, be kind enough to point it out to him? Willie had never seen the place, he told the detective, in his life. He said that Mr. David showed him where it was.

When Willie got to the night of September 14th, 1922, in his testimony his anger and indignation were gone; he was placid, attentive, and courteous. He explained quietly that he had come home for supper that night, had gone to his room afterward, and "remained in the house, leaving it at two-thirty in the morning with my sister." Before he went to bed, he said, he had closed his door to confine to his own room the odor of tobacco smoke from his pipe. "Who objected to that?" asked Mr. Case. Willie gave his sudden, beaming grin. "Everybody," he said, and won the first of several general laughs from the courtroom. Then he told the story of what happened at two-thirty in the morning. It is necessary, for a well-rounded picture of Willie Stevens, to give it here at some length. "I was awakened by my sister knocking at my door," said Willie, "and I immediately rose and went to the door and she said, 'I want you to come down to the church as Edward has not come home; I am very much worried'—or words to that effect. I immediately got dressed and accompanied her down to the church. I went through the front door, followed a small path that led directly to the back of the house past the cellar door. We went directly down Redmond Street to Jones Avenue, from Jones Avenue we went to George Street; turning into George Street we went directly down to Commercial Avenue. There our movements were blocked by an immense big freight automobile. We had to wait there maybe half a minute until it went by, going toward New York.

"I am not at all sure whether we crossed right there at Commercial Avenue or went a little farther down George Street and went diagonally across to the church. Then we stopped there and looked at the church to see whether there were any lights. There were no lights burning. Then Mrs. Hall said, 'We might as well go down and see if it could not be possible that he was at the Mills' house.' We went down there, down George Street until we came to Carman Street, turned down Carman Street, and got in front of the Mills' house and stood there two or three minutes to see if there were any lights in the Mills' apartment. There were none." Willie then described, street by street, the return home, and ended with "I opened the front door with my latchkey. If you wish me, I will show it to you. My sister said, 'You might as well go to bed. You can do no more good.' With that I went upstairs to bed." This was the story that Alexander Simpson had to shake. But before Willie was turned over to him, the witness told how he heard that his brother-in-law had been killed. "I remember I was in the parlor," said Willie, "reading a copy of the *New York Times*. I heard someone coming up the steps and I glanced up and I heard my aunt, Mrs. Charles J. Carpender, say, 'Well, you might as well know it—Edward has been shot.'" Willie's voice was thick with emotion. He was asked what happened then. "Well," he said, "I simply let the paper go—that way" (he let his left hand fall slowly and limply to his side) "and I put my head down, and I cried." Mr. Case asked him if he was present at, or had anything to do with, the murder of Mr. Hall and Mrs. Mills. "Absolutely nothing at all!" boomed Willie, coming out of his posture of sorrow, belligerently erect. The attorney for the defense turned, with a confident little bow, to Alexander Simpson. The special prosecutor sauntered over and stood in front of the witness. Willie took in his breath sharply.

Alexander Simpson, a lawyer, a state senator, slight, perky, capable of harsh tongue-lashings, given to sarcasm and innuendo, had intimated that he would "tie Willie Stevens into knots." Word had gone around that he intended to "flay" the eccentric fellow. Hence his manner now came as a surprise. He spoke in a gentle, almost inaudible voice, and his attitude was one of solicitous friendliness. Willie, quite unexpectedly, drew first blood. Simpson asked him if he had ever earned his livelihood. "For about four or five years," said Willie, "I was employed by Mr. Siebold, a contractor." Not having anticipated an affirmative reply, Simpson paused. Willie leaned forward and said, politely, "Do you wish his address?" He did this in good faith, but the spectators took it for what the *Times* called a "sally," because Simpson had been in the habit of letting loose a swarm of investigators on anyone whose name was brought into the case. "No, thank you," muttered Simpson, above a roar of laughter. The prosecutor now set about picking at Willie's story of the night of September 14th: he tried to find out why the witness and his sister had not knocked on the Mills' door to see if Mr. Hall was there. Unfortunately for the steady drumming of questions, Willie soon broke the prosecutor up with another laugh. Simpson had occasion to mention a New Brunswick boarding house called The Bayard, and he pronounced "Bay" as it is spelled. With easy politeness, Willie corrected him. "*Bi*yard," said Willie. "Biyard?" repeated Simpson. Willie smiled, as at an apt pupil. Simpson bowed slightly. The spectators laughed again.

Presently the witness made a slip, and Simpson pounced on it like a swooping falcon. Asked if he had not, at the scene of the murder, stood "in the light of an automobile while a woman on a mule went by," Willie replied, "I never remember that occurrence." Let us take up the court record from there. "Q.—You would remember if it occurred, wouldn't you? A.—I certainly would, but I don't remember of ever being in an automobile and the light from the automobile shone on a woman on a mule. Q.—Do you say you were not there, or you don't remember? A.—I say positively I was not there. Q.—Why did you say you don't *remember?* A.—Does not that cover the same thing? Q.—No, it don't, because you might be there and not remember it. A.—Well, I will withdraw that, if I may, and say I was not there positively." Willie assumed an air of judicial authority as he "withdrew" his previous answer, and he spoke his positive denial with sharp decision. Mr. Simpson abruptly tried a new tack. "You have had a great deal of experience in life, Mr. Stevens," he said, "and have read a great deal, they say, and know a lot about human affairs. Don't you think it sounds rather fishy when you say you got up in the middle of the night to go and look for Dr. Hall and went to the house and never even knocked on the door—with your experience of human affairs and people that you met and all that sort of thing—don't that seem rather fishy to you?" There was a loud bickering of attorneys before Willie could say anything to this. Finally Judge Parker turned to the witness and said, "Can you answer that, Mr. Stevens?" "The only way I can answer it, Your Honor," said Willie, scornfully, "is that I don't see that it is at all 'fishy.'" The prosecutor jumped to something else: "Dr. Hall's church was not your church, was it?" he asked. "He was not a *Doctor*, sir," said Willie, once more the instructor. "He was the Reverend *Mister* Hall." Simpson paused, nettled. "I am glad you corrected me on that," he said. The courtroom laughed again.

The prosecutor now demanded that Willie repeat his story of what happened at two-thirty. He hoped to establish, he intimated, that the witness had learned it "by rote." Willie calmly went over the whole thing again, in complete detail, but no one of his sentences was the same as it had been. The prosecutor asked him to tell it a third time. The defense objected vehemently. Simpson vehemently objected to the defense's objection. The Court: "We will let him tell it once more." At this point Willie said, "May I say a word?" "Certainly," said Simpson. "Say all you want." Weighing his words carefully, speaking with slow emphasis, Willie said, "All I have to say is I was never taught, as you insinuate, by any person whatsoever. That is my best recollection from the time I started out with my sister to this present minute." Simpson did not insist further on a third recital. He wanted to know now how Willie could establish the truth of his statement that he was in his room from 8 or 9 o'clock until his sister knocked on the door at 2:30 A.M. "Why," said Willie, "if a person sees me go upstairs and does not see me come downstairs, isn't that a conclusion that I was in my room?" The court record shows that Mr. Simpson replied, "Absolutely." "Well," said Willie expansively, "that is all there was to it." Nobody but the pig woman had testified to seeing Willie after he went up to his room that night. Barbara Tough, a servant who had been off during the day, testified that she got back to the Hall home about 10 o'clock and noticed that Willie's door was closed (Willie had testified that it wouldn't stay closed unless he locked it). Louise Geist, of the annulment suit, had testified that she had not seen

Willie that night after dinner. It was Willie's story against the pig woman's. That day in court he overshadowed her. When he stepped down from the witness chair, his shoulders were back and he was smiling broadly. Headlines in the *Times* the next day said, "Willie Stevens Remains Calm Under Cross-Examination. Witness a Great Surprise." There was a touch of admiration, almost of partisanship, in most of the reporters' stories. The final verdict could be read between the lines. The trial dragged on for another ten days, but on the 3rd of December, Willie Stevens was a free man.

He was glad to get home. He stood on the porch of 23 Nichol Avenue, beaming at the house. Reporters had followed him there. He turned to them and said, solemnly, "It is one hundred and four days since I've been here. And I want to get in." They let him go. But two days later, on a Sunday, they came back and Mrs. Hall received them in the drawing room. They could hear Willie in an adjoining room, talking spiritedly. He was, it came out, discussing metallurgy with the Rev. J. Mervin Pettit, who had succeeded Mr. Hall as rector of the Church of St. John the Evangelist.

Willie Stevens, going on seventy, no longer visits the firehouse of No. 3 Engine Company. His old friends have caught only glimpses of him in the past few years, for he has been in feeble health, and spends most of his time in his room, going for a short ride now and then in his chauffeur-driven car. The passerby, glancing casually into the car, would not recognize the famous figure of the middle 1920's. Willie has lost a great deal of weight, and the familiar beaming light no longer comes easily to his eyes.

After Willie had been acquitted and sent home, he tried to pick up the old routine of life where he had left it, but people turned to stare after him in the street, and boys were forever at his heels, shouting, "Look out, Willie, Simpson is after you!" The younger children were fond of him and did not tease him, and once in a while Willie could be seen playing with them, as boisterously and whimsically as ever. The firemen say that if he encountered a ragged child he would find new clothes for it. But Willie's adventures in the streets of the town became fewer and farther apart. Sometimes months would elapse between his visits to the firehouse. When he did show up in his old haunts, he complained of headaches, and while he was still in his fifties, he spent a month in bed with a heart ailment. After that, he stayed close to home, and the firemen rarely saw him. If you should drop by the firehouse, and your interest in Willie seems friendly, they will tell you some fond stories about him.

One winter Willie took a Cook's tour of Hawaii. When he came back, he told the firemen he had joined an organization which, for five dollars, gave its subscribers a closer view of the volcanoes than the ordinary tourist could get. Willie was crazy about the volcanoes. His trip, however, was spoiled, it came out, because someone recognized and pointed him out as the famous Willie Stevens of the Hall-Mills case. He had the Cook's agent cancel a month's reservation at a hotel and rearrange his schedule so that he could leave on the next ship. He is infuriated by any reference to the murders or to the trial. Some years ago a newspaper printed a paragraph about a man out West who was "a perfect double for Willie Stevens." Someone in the firehouse showed it to Willie and he tore the paper to shreds in a rage.

Willie still spends a great deal of time reading "heavy books"—on engineering, on entomology, on botany. Those who have seen his famous room at 23 Nichol Avenue—he has a friend in to visit him once in a while—say that it is filled with books. He has no use for detective stories or the Western and adventure magazines his friends the firemen read. When he is not reading scientific tomes, he dips into the classics or what he calls the "worthwhile poets." He used to astound the firemen with his wide range of knowledge. There was the day a salesman of shaving materials dropped in at the enginehouse. Finding that Willie had visited St. Augustine, Florida, he mentioned an old Spanish chapel there. Willie described it and gave its history, replete with dates, and greatly impressed the caller. Another time someone mentioned a certain kind of insect which he said was found in this country. "You mean they used to be," said Willie.

"That type of insect has been extinct in this country for forty years." It turned out that it had been, too. On still another occasion Willie fell to discussing flowers with some visitor at the firehouse and reeled off a Latin designation—*crassinae carduaceae*, or something of the sort. Then he turned, grinning, to the listening firemen. "Zinnias to you," he said.

Willie Stevens' income from the trust fund established for him is said to be around forty dollars a week. His expenditures are few, now that he is no longer able to go on long trips. The firemen like especially to tell about the time that Willie went to Wyoming, and attended a rodeo. He told the ticket-seller he wanted to sit in a box and the man gave him a single ticket. Willie explained that he wanted the whole box to himself, and he planked down a ten-dollar bill for it. Then he went in and sat in the box all alone. "I had a hell of a time!" he told the firemen gleefully when he came back home.

De Russey's Lane, which Detective David once pointed out to Willie Stevens, is now, you may have heard, entirely changed. Several years ago it was renamed Franklin Boulevard, and where the Rev. Mr. Edward W. Hall and Mrs. Eleanor Mills lay murdered there is now a row of neat brick and stucco houses. The famous crab apple tree under which the bodies were found disappeared the first weekend after the murders. It was hacked to pieces, roots and all, by souvenir-hunters.

The Remarkable Case
of Mr. Bruhl

SAMUEL O. BRUHL was just an ordinary-looking citizen, like you and me, except for a curious, shoe-shaped scar on his left cheek, which he got when he fell against a wagon-tongue in his youth. He had a good job as treasurer for a syrup-and-fondant concern, a large, devout wife, two tractable daughters, and a nice home in Brooklyn. He worked from nine to five, took in a show occasionally, played a bad, complacent game of golf, and was usually in bed by eleven o'clock. The Bruhls had a dog named Bert, a small circle of friends, and an old sedan. They had made a comfortable, if unexciting, adjustment to life.

There was no reason in the world why Samuel Bruhl shouldn't have lived along quietly until he died of some commonplace malady. He was a man designed by Nature for an uneventful life, an inexpensive but respectable funeral, and a modest stone marker. All this you would have predicted had you observed his colorless comings and goings, his mild manner, the small stature of his dreams. He was, in brief, the sort of average citizen that observers of Judd Gray thought Judd Gray was. And precisely as that mild little family man was abruptly hurled into an incongruous tragedy, so was Samuel Bruhl suddenly picked out of the hundreds of men just like him and marked for an extravagant and unpredictable end. Oddly enough it was the shoe-shaped scar on his left cheek which brought to his heels a Nemesis he had never dreamed of. A blemish on his heart, a tic in his soul would have been different; one would have blamed Bruhl for whatever anguish an emotional or spiritual flaw laid him open to, but it is ironical indeed when the Furies ride down a man who has been guilty of nothing worse than an accident in his childhood.

Samuel O. Bruhl looked very much like George ("Shoescar") Clinigan. Clinigan had that same singular shoe-shaped scar on his left cheek. There was also a general resemblance in height, weight, and complexion. A careful study would have revealed very soon that Clinigan's eyes were shifty and Bruhl's eyes were clear, and that the syrup-and-fondant company's treasurer had a more pleasant mouth and a higher forehead than the gangster and racketeer, but at a glance the similarity was remarkable.

Had Clinigan not become notorious, this prank of Nature would never have been detected, but Clinigan did become notorious and dozens of persons observed that he looked like Bruhl. They saw Clinigan's picture in the papers the day he was shot, and the day after, and the day after that. Presently someone in the syrup-and-fondant concern mentioned to someone else that Clinigan looked like Mr. Bruhl, remarkably like Mr. Bruhl. Soon everybody in the place had commented on it, among themselves, and to Mr. Bruhl.

Mr. Bruhl rather laughed it off at first, but one day when Clinigan had been in the hospital a week, a cop peered closely at Mr. Bruhl when he was on his way home from work. After that, the little treasurer noticed a number of other strangers staring at him with mingled surprise and alarm. One small, dark man hastily thrust a hand into his coat pocket and paled slightly.

Mr. Bruhl began to worry. He began to imagine things. "I hope this fellow Clinigan doesn't pull through," he said one morning at breakfast. "He's a bad actor. He's better off dead."

"Oh, he'll pull through," said Mrs. Bruhl, who had been reading the morning paper. "It says here he'll pull through. But it says they'll shoot him again. It says they're sure to shoot him again."

The morning after the night that Clinigan left the hospital, secretly, by a side door, and disappeared into the town, Bruhl decided not to go to work. "I don't feel so good today," he said to his wife. "Would you call up the office and tell them I'm sick?"

"You don't look well," said his wife. "You really don't look well. Get down, Bert," she added, for the dog had jumped upon her lap and whined. The animal knew that something was wrong.

That evening Bruhl, who had mooned about the house all day, read in the papers that Clinigan had vanished, but was believed to be somewhere in the city. His various rackets required his presence, at least until he made enough money to skip out with; he had left the hospital penniless. Rival gangsters, the papers said, were sure to seek him out, to hunt him down, to give it to him again. "Give him what again?" asked Mrs. Bruhl when she read this. "Let's talk about something else," said her husband.

It was little Joey, the office-boy at the syrup-and-fondant company, who first discovered that Mr. Bruhl was afraid. Joey, who went about with tennis shoes on, entered the treasurer's office suddenly—flung open the door and started to say something. "Good God!" cried Mr. Bruhl, rising from his chair. "Why, what's the matter, Mr. Bruhl?" asked Joey. Other little things happened. The switchboard girl phoned Mr. Bruhl's desk one afternoon and said there was a man waiting to see him, a Mr. Globe. "What's he look like?" asked Bruhl, who didn't know anybody named Globe. "He's small and dark," said the girl. "A small, dark man?" said Bruhl. "Tell him I'm out. Tell him I've gone to California." The personnel, comparing notes, decided at length that the treasurer was afraid of being mistaken for Shoescar and put on the spot. They said nothing to Mr. Bruhl about this, because they were forbidden to by Ollie Breithofter, a fattish clerk who was a tireless and inventive practical joker and who had an idea.

As the hunt went on for Clinigan and he still wasn't found and killed, Mr. Bruhl lost weight and grew extremely fidgety. He began to figure out new ways of getting to work, one requiring the use of two different ferry lines; he ate his lunch in, he wouldn't answer bells, he cried out when anyone dropped anything, and he ran into stores or banks when cruising taxidrivers shouted at him. One morning, in setting the house to rights, Mrs. Bruhl found a revolver under his pillow. "I found a revolver under your pillow," she told him that night. "Burglars are bad in this neighborhood," he said. "You oughtn't to have a revolver," she said. They argued about it, he irritably, she uneasily, until time for bed. As Bruhl was undressing, after locking and bolting all the doors, the telephone rang. "It's for you, Sam," said Mrs. Bruhl. Her husband went slowly to the phone, passing Bert on the way. "I wish I was you," he said to the dog, and took up the receiver. "Get this, Shoescar," said a husky voice. "We trailed you where you are, see? You're cooked." The receiver at the other end was hung up. Bruhl shouted. His wife came running. "What is it, Sam, what is it?" she cried. Bruhl, pale, sick-looking, had fallen into a chair. "They got me," he moaned. "They got me." Slowly, deviously, Minnie Bruhl got it out of her husband that he had been mistaken for Clinigan and that he was cooked. Mrs. Bruhl was not very quick mentally, but she had a certain intuition and this intuition told her, as she trembled there in her nightgown above her broken husband, that this was the work of Ollie Breithofter. She instantly phoned Ollie Breithofter's wife and, before she hung up, had got the truth out of Mrs. Breithofter. It was Ollie who had called.

The treasurer of the Maskonsett Syrup & Fondant Company, Inc., was so relieved to know that the gangs weren't after him that he admitted frankly at the office next day that Ollie had fooled him for a minute. Mr. Bruhl even joined in the laughter and wisecracking, which went on all day. After that, for almost a week, the mild little man had comparative peace of mind. The papers said very little about Clinigan now. He had completely disappeared. Gang warfare had died down for the time being.

One Sunday morning Mr. Bruhl went for an automobile ride with his wife and daughters. They had driven about a mile through Brooklyn streets when, glancing in the mirror above his

head, Mr. Bruhl observed a blue sedan just behind him. He turned off into the next side street, and the sedan turned off too. Bruhl made another turn, and the sedan followed him. "Where are you going, dear?" asked Mrs. Bruhl. Mr. Bruhl didn't answer her, he speeded up, he drove terrifically fast, he turned corners so wildly that the rear wheels swung around. A traffic cop shrilled at him. The younger daughter screamed. Bruhl drove right on, weaving in and out. Mrs. Bruhl began to berate him wildly. "Have you lost your mind, Sam?" she shouted. Mr. Bruhl looked behind him. The sedan was no longer to be seen. He slowed up. "Let's go home," he said. "I've had enough of this."

A month went by without incident (thanks largely to Mrs. Breithofter) and Samuel Bruhl began to be himself again. On the day that he was practically normal once more, Sluggy Pensiotta, alias Killer Lewis, alias Stranger Koetschke, was shot. Sluggy was the leader of the gang that had sworn to get Shoescar Clinigan. The papers instantly took up the gang-war story where they had left off. Pictures of Clinigan were published again. The slaying of Pensiotta, said the papers, meant but one thing: it meant that Shoescar Clinigan was cooked. Mr. Bruhl, reading this, went gradually to pieces once more.

After another week of skulking about, starting at every noise, and once almost fainting when an automobile backfired near him, Samuel Bruhl began to take on a remarkable new appearance. He talked out of the corner of his mouth, his eyes grew shifty. He looked more and more like Shoescar Clinigan. He snarled at his wife. Once her called her "Babe," and he had never called her anything but Minnie. He kissed her in a strange, new way, acting rough, almost brutal. At the office he was mean and overbearing. He used peculiar language. One night when the Bruhls had friends in for bridge—old Mr. Creegan and his wife—Bruhl suddenly appeared from upstairs with a pair of scarlet pajamas on, smoking a cigarette, and gripping his revolver. After a few loud and incoherent remarks of a boastful nature, he let fly at a clock on the mantel, and hit it squarely in the middle. Mrs. Bruhl screamed. Mr. Creegan fainted. Bert, who was in the kitchen, howled. "What's the matta you?" snarled Bruhl. "Ya bunch of softies."

Quite by accident, Mrs. Bruhl discovered, hidden away in a closet, eight or ten books on gangs and gangsters, which Bruhl had put there. They included *Al Capone, You Can't Win, 10,000 Public Enemies,* and a lot of others; and they were all well thumbed. Mrs. Bruhl realized that it was high time something was done, and she determined to have a doctor for her husband. For two or three days Bruhl had not gone to work. He lay around in his bedroom, in his red pajamas, smoking cigarettes. The office phoned once or twice. When Mrs. Bruhl urged him to get up and dress and go to work, he laughed and patted her roughly on the head. "It's a knockover, kid," he said. "We'll be sitting pretty. To hell with it."

The doctor who finally came and slipped into Bruhl's bedroom was very grave when he emerged. "This is a psychosis," he said, "a definite psychosis. Your husband is living in a world of fantasy. He has built up a curious defense mechanism against something or other." The doctor suggested that a psychiatrist be called in, but after he had gone Mrs. Bruhl decided to take her husband out of town on a trip. The Maskonsett Syrup & Fondant Company, Inc., was very fine about it. Mr. Scully said of course. "Sam is very valuable to us, Mrs. Bruhl," said Mr. Scully, "and we all hope he'll be all right." Just the same he had Mr. Bruhl's accounts examined, when Mrs. Bruhl had gone.

Oddly enough, Samuel Bruhl was amenable to the idea of going away. "I need a rest," he said. "You're right. Let's get the hell out of here." He seemed normal up to the time they set out for the Grand Central and then he insisted on leaving from the 125th Street station. Mrs. Bruhl took exception to this, as being ridiculous, whereupon her doting husband snarled at her. "God, what a dumb moll *I* picked," he said to Minnie Bruhl, and he added bitterly that if the heat was put to him it would be his own babe who was to blame. "And what do you think of *that?*" he said, pushing her to the floor of the cab.

They went to a little inn in the mountains. It wasn't a very nice place, but the rooms were clean and the meals were good. There was no form of entertainment, except a Tom Thumb golf course and an uneven tennis court, but Mr. Bruhl didn't mind. He said it was too cold outdoors, anyway. He stayed indoors, reading and smoking. In the evening he played the mechanical piano in the dining-room. He liked to play "More Than You Know" over and over again. One night, about nine o'clock, he was putting in his seventh or eighth nickel when four men walked into the dining-room. They were silent men, wearing overcoats, and carrying what appeared to be cases for musical instruments. They took out various kinds of guns from their cases, quickly, expertly, and walked over toward Bruhl, keeping step. He turned just in time to see them line up four abreast and aim at him. Nobody else was in the room. There was a cumulative roar and a series of flashes. Mr. Bruhl fell and the men walked out in single file, rapidly, nobody having said a word.

Mrs. Bruhl, state police, and the hotel manager tried to get the wounded man to talk. Chief Witznitz of the nearest town's police force tried it. It was no good. Bruhl only snarled and told them to go away and let him alone. Finally, Commissioner O'Donnell of the New York City Police Department arrived at the hospital. He asked Bruhl what the men looked like. "I don't know what they looked like," snarled Bruhl, "and if I did know I wouldn't tell you." He was silent a moment, then: "Cop!" he added, bitterly. The Commissioner sighed and turned away. "They're all like that," he said to the others in the room. "They never talk." Hearing this, Mr. Bruhl smiled, a pleased smile, and closed his eyes.

The Little Girl
and the Wolf

ONE AFTERNOON a big wolf waited in a dark forest for a little girl to come along carrying a basket of food to her grandmother. Finally a little girl did come along and she was carrying a basket of food. "Are you carrying that basket to your grandmother?" asked the wolf. The little girl said yes, she was. So the wolf asked her where her grandmother lived and the little girl told him and he disappeared into the wood.

When the little girl opened the door of her grandmother's house she saw that there was somebody in bed with a nightcap and nightgown on. She had approached no nearer than twenty-five feet from the bed when she saw that it was not her grandmother but the wolf, for even in a nightcap a wolf does not look any more like your grandmother than the Metro-Goldwyn lion looks like Calvin Coolidge. So the little girl took an automatic out of her basket and shot the wolf dead.

Moral: It is not so easy to fool little girls nowadays as it used to be.

Gang War, 1940*

(From a newspaper account of that day)

POLICE COMMISSIONER MCNAMARA today called upon William A. ("Body Squeaks") McGloin at the racketeer's suite in the Astor-Plaza, and held a long conference. He declined to discuss the nature of their conversation when he emerged at the end of an hour. "We had a very pleasant chat," the Commissioner said. This leaves the killing of Joseph Hawthorne, or Joseph Clusco, just where it was three weeks ago today when he was found in a field in Flatbush.

Commissioner McNamara said he intended to put a stop to the rapidly growing list of witnesses and suspects, which now includes, in addition to those whose names have already been printed, Boston Sammy, Jack of Diamonds Nellihan, Mr. and Mrs. J. Carter Montgomery, Yolande Neilson, the actress, Commissioner of Records Charles E. Daul, Detective Richard Groarty, George O. ("Breathed His Last") Callahan, and Mr. and Mrs. Damon E. Prince and daughter Gloria.

"We now have some eighty or ninety suspects," said McNamara, "and that is almost enough to do us through the summer. This is by far the largest number of suspects and witnesses we have ever gathered together for a gangster murder. They have

*Written in 1929

36

told some very interesting, though conflicting, stories, and almost every suspect photographs well. I believe I may say that the rotogravure editors are well satisfied with the progress we have made." The Commissioner added that he thought the most important development today was the change in Boston Sammy's story. "Boston has maintained that he saw Hawthorne get into the automobile but did not see him being called to the telephone," said McNamara. "Now he says that he did not see him get into the automobile but that he did see him go to the telephone. Makes interesting reading."

Those close to the Commissioner believe that he intends to drop the case as soon as the total number of suspects reaches an even hundred. It is known that McGloin has been very generous in suggesting possible suspects to McNamara, and their conference today may have been for the purpose of getting a few more good names before putting an end to the probe. Friends of McGloin say that he is about ready for the investigation to be closed. "McGloin is getting pretty tired of police interference," said one of his friends today. "His secretaries are constantly being annoyed by sergeants and lieutenants who wish interviews with him. McGloin is too busy to be a suspect and it is futile for the police to try to get him to act in that capacity. Every time he has been a suspect in a murder case, even where the victim was some rival whom McGloin had sworn to take for a ride, the investigation has come to nothing. It simply leads to bad feeling all around."

One rumor today had it that McGloin would confess if he received assurance of a good enough "break" in the newspapers. It is doubtful if he would get much attention with another confession, however, because his last three have all been much the same, ending with his repudiation of each story on the ground that he was temporarily deranged when he confessed, and the novelty has considerably worn off.

The statements of friends, that McGloin is growing tired of the Hawthorne investigation, tally with what the racketeer told a reporter for this paper yesterday. "I'm too greatly tied up with the Bronx beer situation to spend much time on this probe," said

McGloin. "I understand of course that Commissioner McNamara has to do something about the murderers of prominent racketeers and gamblers, but what more does he want in this case? True, I haven't confessed, but I've given the Commissioner the names of a couple dozen colorful characters to arrest, all of whom are willing to talk, one way or another. Boston Sammy alone can make up more interesting stories about seeing victims telephoning, and so on, than all the suspects put together since the Rothstein case."

It is expected in police and racketeering circles that McNamara and McGloin will compromise on dropping the case by the first of the month. McNamara has asked for a good play in the newspapers, particularly the picture-papers, on this case, and he has had it. Boston Sammy and Yolande Neilson alone have been photographed several dozen times. Miss Neilson today signed a contract with a weekly magazine to do a series of articles on "What I Know About the Man Who Killed Hawthorne." Commissioner McNamara has agreed to allow her first article to appear in print, before he questions her himself, on the ground that it would be unfair to her if her revelations were given to the newspapers, through his office, before the series of articles began running.

"The fact that Miss Neilson's tale indicates that it was a man, and not a woman, who did the shooting is interesting," said Commissioner McNamara today, in commenting on the case. "I shall eagerly await her stories, especially those in which she tells the name of the murderer. We ought to have that."

The Imperturbable Spirit

M R. MONROE stood fingering some canes in a shop in the Fifties. Canes, it occurred to him, were imperturbable. He liked that adjective, which he had been encountering in a book he was reading on God, ethics, morals, humanism, and so on. The word stood staunch, like a bulwark, rumbled, like a caisson. Mr. Monroe was pleased to find himself dealing in similes.

He finally decided not to buy a cane. Mrs. Monroe was arriving that afternoon on the *Leviathan* and he would need both hands to wave porters around on the dock. His wife had to be looked after. She was such a child. When imperturbability was at the flood in Mr. Monroe, his wife's nature took on for him a curiously dependent and childlike quality, not at all annoying, considerably endearing, and wholly mythical.

From the cane shop Mr. Monroe wandered to a bookstore. On his imperturbable days it was almost impossible for him to work. He liked to brood and reflect and occasionally to catch glimpses of himself in store windows, slot-machine mirrors, etc., brooding and reflecting. He bought a paperback novel, in the original French, by André Maurois. The gesture—it was purely that for the simple reason that he did not read French—added a vague fillip to his day. Then he walked part way up Fifth Avenue, in the brisk air, and finally hailed a cab.

When he got home he took a bath, put on clean linen and another suit, and sank into a great chair to read some more in the book on God, morals, and so on. In the course of this he looked up three words in a dictionary, *eschatological, maleficent,* and *teleology.* He read the definition of the last word twice, frowned, and let it go. Despite the fact that the outlook for mankind was far from bright in the particular chapter he was reading, Mr. Monroe began to feel pretty much the master of his fate. Nonfiction, of a philosophical nature, always affected him that way, regardless of its content.

Mr. Monroe wandered leisurely about the pier, complimenting himself on having remembered to get a customs pass, and on the way his mind kept dealing in interesting ideas. With an imperturbable frown, he watched the big liner nosing in. Did fog at sea imply a malign aspect of the cosmos? If it came and went, without incident, did that connote luck, or what? Suppose it shielded an iceberg which sank the ship—did that prove the existence of an antic Malice? Mr. Monroe liked the word antic. "Antic," he said, half aloud. He wondered vaguely if he, too, should not write a book about morals, malice, menace, and so on, showing how they could be handled by the imperturbable spirit. . . .

Little Mrs. Monroe, burdened with coats and bundles, rosy, lovely, at length appeared. Mr. Monroe's heart leapt up, but at the same time he set himself as if to receive a service in tennis. He remembered (oh, keenly) as he stepped toward her, how she was wont to regard him as a person likely to "go to pieces" over trifles. Well, she would find him a changed man. He kissed her warmly, but withal in such a strangely masterful manner, that she was at first a little surprised—a tennis player taken aback by a sudden change in the tactics of an old, old opponent. In three minutes of backcourt rallying she figured out that he had been reading something, but she said nothing. She let his lobs go unkilled.

When Mrs. Monroe stood in line at the desk where they assign inspectors, he offered to take her place. "No, no," she whispered.

"Just pretend you're not with me. It'll be easier." A slow pallor came upon Mr. Monroe's face.

"Whatta y' got?" he croaked.

"A dozen bottles of Benedictine," she breathed.

"Oh my God!" said Mr. Monroe, dropping, figuratively, his racquet.

An inspector stepped forward and stood waiting.

"So glad," murmured Mrs. Monroe to her husband, collectedly, as to a casual acquaintance. Mr. Monroe fumbled at his hat, and wandered away, tugging at the left sleeve of his coat, a nervous gesture of his. She'd never get away with it. Twelve bottles! Quarts, probably, or magnums—no, it didn't come that way. Well, it came in big, bulky bottles anyway. Let's see, hadn't a new conspiracy law come in? Couldn't they send you to jail now? He could see himself in court, being flayed by a state's attorney. Mr. Monroe had a phobia about law-breaking, even about ordinance-breaking. . . . "Now, gentlemen of the jury . . ." The state's attorney put on his nose glasses, brought out a letter and read it in nasty, slow accents, a horrible, damning letter, which Mr.

Monroe had never seen before, but which, fiendishly enough, *was in his own handwriting.* The jury stirred.

"Now wait a minute—" began Mr. Monroe, aloud.

"What *are* you talking about?" demanded his wife.

The courtroom mercifully faded. Mr. Monroe turned and stared at his wife. "Ah—ha, dear!" he said, thickly. "I'm all through!" she said, brightly. "Let's go home."

By the time they reached their house, Mr. Monroe was his old self, or rather his new self, again. He had even pretty well persuaded himself that his iron nerve had got the Benedictine through the customs. His strange, masterful manner came back. No sooner had he got into his slippers, however, and reached for his book, than Mrs. Monroe, in the next room, emitted a small squeal. "My hatbox!" she cried. "We left it at the dock!"

"Oh, damn! damn!" said Mr. Monroe. "Well, I'll have to go back after it, that's all. What was in it?"

*They were really porters, but Mr. Monroe
thought they were guards.*

"Some cute hats I got for almost nothing and—well, that's about all."

"*About* all?"

"Well, three of the bottles."

Mr. Monroe squealed, in turn. "Ah, God," he said, bitterly.

"There's nothing to be afraid of now, silly," his wife said. "They were passed through!"

"I'm not afraid; I'll handle this," murmured her husband.

In a sort of stupor he went out, hailed a cab, and climbed in. Life got you. A scheme of morals? A shield against menace? What good did that do? Impertur—ha! Menace got you—no bigger than a man's hand at first, no bigger than a hatbox. . . . "Now, gentlemen of the jury . . . conspiracy . . . defraud the government . . . seditious . . ."

Mr. Monroe crept whitely through the wide street entrance to the docks. The last stragglers were piling baggage into taxis in the noisy channel beyond. A few suitcases and boxes were still coming down the traveling platform from the dock level above. At the bottom, where they tumbled in a heap, two guards stood to receive them. They were really porters, but Mr. Monroe thought they were guards. They had big jaws. One of them gradually turned into a state's attorney before Mr. Monroe's very eyes! The stricken husband wandered idly over to the other side of the moving platform. There stood a lonely, sinister hatbox, a trap, a pitfall, Exhibit A. "Now, gentlemen . . ."

"That your box, brother?" asked the state's attorney.

"Oh, no," said Mr. Monroe, "nope." The porter seemed disappointed. Mr. Monroe walked out into the channel where the taxis were. Then he walked back again; out again; and back again. The guards had turned away and were fussing with a trunk. Mr. Monroe trembled. He walked stiffly to the hatbox, picked it up, and walked stiffly through the doorway, out into the street.

"Hey!" cried a loud voice. Mr. Monroe broke into a run. "Taxi!" continued the loud voice. But Mr. Monroe was a hundred yards away. He ran three blocks without stopping, walked half a

block, and ran again. He came home by a devious route, rested for
a while outside his door, and went in. . . .

That night Mr. Monroe read to his wife from the morals, ethics,
and imperturbability book. He read in a deep, impressive voice,
and slowly, for there was a lot his wife wouldn't grasp at once.

American Folk Dance.

"Perhaps this will refresh your memory."

"Have you people got any .38 cartridges?"

"Have you no code, man?"

*"In first-aid class today we learned eleven different ways
to poison people."*

"It's in de Bag for de Little Guy, Bobby."

"Have you fordotten our ittle suicide pact?"

"I'm the Times *man. Did they have pistol permits?"*

Hell Only Breaks Loose Once

(Written after reading James M. Cain's The Postman Always Rings Twice)

I

THEY KICKED me out of college when I was about twenty-seven. I went up to see the Dean and tried to hand him a couple of laughs but it was no good. He said he couldn't put me back in college but I could hang around the office and sweep out and wash windows. I figured I better be rambling and I said I had a couple of other offers. He told me to sit down and think it over so I sat down.

Then she came in the room. She was tall and thin and had a white frowning forehead and soft eyes. She wasn't much to look at but she was something to think about. As far as she and I were concerned he wasn't in the room. She leaned over the chair where I was sitting and bit me in the ear. I let her have it right under the heart. It was a good one. It was plenty. She hit the floor like a two-year-old.

"What fell?" asked the Dean, peering over his glasses. I told him nothing fell.

II

After a while I said I guessed I'd hang around and go to work for him. "Do what?" he asked. He had forgot all about me, but I hung around. I liked him and he liked me but neither one of us cared what happened to the other.

When the Dean went out to lunch I walked into a rear office and she was there. I began to tremble all over like a hooch dancer. She was fussing with some papers but I could see she wasn't really doing anything. I walked close to her. It was like dying and going to Heaven. She was a little like my mother and a little like the time I got my hip busted in a football scrimmage. I reached over and let her have one on the chin and she went down like a tray of dishes. I knew then I would be beating her up the rest of my life. It made me feel like it was April and I was a kid again and had got up on a warm morning and it was all misty outdoors and the birds were singing.

III

"Hi, Dean," I said to him when he got back from lunch.

"What is it?" he asked. I could tell he thought he had never seen me before. I told him what it was. "Excellent," he said, looking surprised. He still didn't know what it was. She came out of the back room and he asked her what she wanted. He never remembered seeing anybody.

I took her out to lunch. It was sweet in the lunchroom and I kicked her under the table and broke her ankle. It was still broken when I carried her back to the Dean's office.

"Who do you wish to see?" he asked, looking over his glasses at us. I wanted to grind his glasses into his skull. She said we both worked there. He said that was excellent, but he wasn't looking for work. I told him to think it over and she and I went into the back room. I let her have one over the eye but it was a glancing blow and didn't knock her out. She cracked down on me with a paperweight and I went out like a light but I took her with me. She broke her head in the fall. We were unconscious for about an hour. A couple of guys were bending over us when we came to. They said they were from a place named Lang's, a cleaning establishment. The Dean had got the idea we were a bear rug and was going to send us out to be dry-cleaned. He was pretty dumb but I liked him.

IV

"What do you want to work for that guy for?"

"I'm his secretary."

"What do you want to work for him for?"

"I said I'm his secretary."

"Keep talking."

"I have to work for him. He's my husband." I felt pretty sick then.

"That's tough. You oughtn't to be married to him. He doesn't know what it's all about."

"He lectures in his sleep."

"That must be swell."

"I don't want to be his wife. I want to be yours."

"You are mine."

"Let me have it again," she said. I gave her a short left jab on the button. She was dizzy for days.

V

The Dean was too absentminded to notice she was bruised all the time. It made me sick seeing him sitting at his desk trying to remember what it was all about. One day he began dictating a letter to me but I didn't pay any attention. I went on dusting a chair. Pretty soon he went out to lunch and I went in the back room. She was there and I began to shiver like a tuning fork. I stroked her hair. I had never done that before. It was like going to sleep.

"There is one out for us," she told me.

"Okay," I said.

VI

He was sitting at his desk trying to figure out who he was when I hit him over the conk with an auto crank. I thought he would fold up like a leather belt, but he didn't. It didn't faze him. "Somebody's at the door," he said. I was shaking a little but I went to the door and opened it. There wasn't anybody there. I stood to one side so he could look out of the door into the hall. It was empty. "I thought I heard somebody knock," he said. It made me cold.

VII

We fixed him finally. I got him up on top of the university water tower one night to see the aurora borealis. There wasn't any aurora borealis but he was too dumb to notice that. It was swell up there on the tower. It smelled pretty. It smelled of jasmine. I felt like the first time I ever kissed a girl.

I rigged up one of those double flights of steps like tap-dancers dance up and down on and told him to get up on top of it.

"I don't want to get up on top of that," he said.

"You want to see the aurora borealis, don't you?"

"Most certainly."

"Then get up on top of that."

He got up on top of it and I climbed up after him. The thing was rickety but he didn't notice.

"What are we doing up here?" he asked me.

"Look at the aurora," I said, pointing at the sky. He looked and while we were standing there she came up on top of the steps with us. He didn't pay any attention to her. I swayed from side to side and started the thing teetering. I beat her up a little and then I beat him up a little. He looked like he had been spanked by an old aunt. The thing was swinging bad now, from one side to the other. I knew it was going over.

VIII

We all fell six flights. He was dead when they picked him up. She was dead too. I was near to her, but she was a long way off. I was dying, they told me. So I dictated this to a guy from the D.A.'s office, and here it is. And that's all, except I hope it's pretty in Heaven and smells like when the lilacs first come out on May nights in the Parc Monceau in Paris.

Izzy and Moe

F EW RESIDENTS of this naughty city have to scratch their heads to recall the Messrs. Izzy Einstein and Moe W. Smith—that is, if they hear the two gentlemen alluded to simply as Izzy and Moe. For the benefit of the very young, however, and of strangers in town, it may be said that Izzy and Moe were the most famous of prohibition-enforcement agents in this area of scofflaws. Beginning more than fifteen years ago, the twain were accustomed to knock off, as Moe once put it, fifteen to twenty joints a week—some weeks, as many as a hundred. These joints were violating the laws of the land and thereby laid themselves open to being knocked off, in the name of the government at Washington.

"When we made an arrest, we told dem politely, 'Dere's sad news here,'" Izzy will tell you. The two federal agents, who worked together, broke the sad news to, in all, more than forty-six hundred people. The recipients of the mournful tidings, brought by the 250-pound Moe and the only slightly lighter Izzy, ranged from gentlemanly proprietors of country-club bars to tough guys selling "smoke" in dives.

The newspapers, always on the lookout for picturesque figures, began to play up, scoffingly at first, the raids of the two Jewish officers, always referring to them as Izzy and Moe because there was a laugh in it and because the names fit snugly into the headlines. The Messrs. Einstein and Smith liked the publicity and got a great kick out of being called plain Izzy and Moe. Moe's business cards today bear this legend in the lower left-hand corner:

FORMERLY WITH
U. S. GOVT. "PROHIBITION"
IZZY AND MOE

The quotation marks are Moe's, but they carry no intentional irony, for Izzy and Moe's prohibition did prohibit; they always got their man even if they had to disguise themselves to get into this club or that joint.

When they raided a golf club they wore knickers and carried a niblick or two, and when they called on the dives they dressed roughly, like teamsters or stevedores; now and again they donned evening clothes to gain entry to a smart *boîte de nuit*. They were never Hindu princes or Russian dancers or anything of that sort, but tall tales of their daring and ingenious costumes have passed into the colorful legend of Baghdad on the Dubway.

Their work was not romantic to them, Moe says; it was just a job for which each of them got $3,600 a year. Toward the end of 1925 it was announced that they would retire from government service, for the reason that they were so widely known that their usefulness was over. Moe got out then, but Izzy, because of his fluency in Yiddish, was retained another year to investigate rabbinical wine scandals.

They had had their adventures, but they had only once been in a rough-and-tumble fight and had fired only two shots during their five years of raiding. The fight occurred when Izzy tried to arrest two Polish brothers who ran a Third Avenue saloon. The wives of the Poles began to lambast Izzy with a mop and a broom, and Moe, rushing to the rescue, socked one of the men on the jaw and laid him out. (Moe was a pugilist in his youth, fighting as a featherweight, of all weights. He weighed then 126, just about half of what he weighs now.) Moe could not bring himself to clip the women on the chin, however, and they were rapidly getting the best of the situation when Izzy ran out and called the cops.

As for the shooting, it occurred at a garage in Yonkers when a man who was quietly distilling there nervously slammed a door on Izzy's arm. Moe impetuously let fly two shots. Nobody was hit.

So much for the good old days. The sight of Izzy or Moe or both of them looming up on a man's threshold nowadays still may disturb the man, but not for the same reason as in the era of the noble experiment. Izzy and Moe are both insurance agents now, and they both work for the New York Life Insurance Company; furthermore, they both belong to that company's "400 Club," which means that they are among the top salesmen—high-pressure, live-wire go-getters who write at least $400,000 worth of business a year. Each of the former raiders has sold policies to half a dozen men whom they once arrested. They both work hard at it and are about equally successful.

Izzy says that he frequently meets gentlemen whom he used to arrest. "If you have arrested forty-six hundred people, you're running into 'em here and there. And they're greeting me very kindly. 'Hi, Izzy,' they say."

Izzy enjoys telling the story of one of his hundreds of arrests. It seems that he sauntered in to a restaurant on Broadway one morning, bought some liquor, and told the waiter he was under arrest. The waiter pleaded to be allowed to telephone his boss, the owner of the restaurant, and tell him to come around. Izzy said that would be O.K. if the fellow hurried up.

The fellow hurried up, all right; he was on hand in a few minutes, his shoes unlaced and his tie untied. He began calling Izzy by his name. "Don't you know *me?*" asked the man.

"I never seen you before," said Izzy.

"Well," said the man, hopefully, "ain't your wife's name Esther?" Izzy admitted that it was. "An' she lived on Stanton Street, and her fadder's name was Morris Sattler?"

"Dis is perfectly O.K.," said Izzy, "but how are you knowing?"

"Well, I almost married Esther," said the man.

"So," Izzy told us, "I gave him his punishment."

Izzy and Moe are still friends, although four years ago there was a little incident that threatened to disrupt their friendhsip. Moe heard that Izzy was working on a book to be called *Prohibition Agent No. 1*, so he informed Izzy and Izzy's publishers that if he (Moe) was mentioned in the book, he would bring an action. Since Izzy called himself Agent No. 1, that made Moe by inference Agent No. 2, and he didn't want any part of that.

So Izzy cut out all references to Moe by name, and the incident ended amiably enough. The book sold 575 copies. "The publishers sent me a free copy," said Moe. "Izzy would have sent me a copy too, if I had sent him two dollars."

How the Kooks Crumble

I AM NOW CONVINCED that American radio, or what is left of it, is unconsciously intent (I hope it's unconsciously) upon driving such of its listeners as are not already kooky, kooky. Before we proceed with the indictment, let's examine the slang noun *kook*, from which the adjective *kooky* is derived. The newest *Dictionary of American Slang* has this to say about kook: "n. An odd, eccentric, disliked person; a 'drip'; a nut. Teenage use since 1958; rapidly becoming a pop. fad word. Kooky, adj. crazy, nuts; odd, eccentric; having the attributes of a 'drip.'"

It seems to me that the *Dictionary of American Slang* is a little odd or eccentric (I don't say crazy or nuts) when it fails to trace *kook* and *kooky* to the much older slang word *cuckoo* or *coo-coo*. It might also have pointed out the possibility that the new word derives from Kukla of the old Kukla, Fran, and Ollie television program. According to the slang dictionary, the female European cuckoo is the bird that lays its eggs in another bird's nest, which may be odd or eccentric, but, as any mother will tell you, is by no means crazy or nuts. The American female cuckoo, by the way, hatches its own eggs in its own nest—but let's not get so deeply into this that we can't get out.

My indictment of radio, to return to that, is aimed specifically at most of the news reporters, or reporters of bad news, to be exact. These men seem to revel in news items of horror, terror, catastrophe, and calamity. I have forced myself to listen, during the past few months, to an assortment of these voices of doom which are heard all day long, on the hour or half-hour, over almost all radio stations. It is something in the nature of a God's blessing to cut them off and turn to the intelligent programs on WNYC and music of WQXR. It is wonderful to get away from the yelling and howling of what might be called the present-day Creepy Time melodies and lyrics (and I apologize to both of those fine words). One of these gibberings poses the question, "What is love?" and answers it with "Five feet of heaven in a pony tail."

But let's get back to those reporters of disaster and death. Most of them seem to have been taught diction, phrasing, and mono-tone in two separate schools for announcers. One group of these men presents the horror of fires, automobile accidents, and multiple family murders in a tone of incongruous and chilling, matter-of-fact calm. The other group leaps upon items of daily terror in a mindless tone of almost eager elation. Let us glance, for as long as we can stand it, at the formula of one of these broadcasts of daily American hell. This kind of program usually lasts fifteen minutes, begins on a high note of cataclysm, and ends with a report of "stocks and the weather." In between, there are often as many as five or six commercials, and in many instances these are read by the reporters themselves in exactly the same tone as the calamities, thus giving the listener the spooky feeling that the deaths of scores of persons in an aircrash are no more important than a new candy bar or brand of coffee. But let me set down a mild paraphrase of the broadcasts I am indicting:

"Thirty-seven persons were killed today, and more than one hundred others critically injured, in a chain collision of some twenty-five pleasure cars and trucks on a fog-bound New Jersey highway. Mrs. Marcia Kook, who yesterday shot down eleven members of her family with two double-barreled shotguns, was killed today by her estranged husband, who also took the lives of the couple next door, a mortician out walking his dog, two school teachers, and a nun. Police say that they found two million dollars' worth of heroin fastened to her underclothing. Do you know the true glory of gracious modern living? You don't unless you have tried Becker's Butternut Coffee with that serene, heavenly flavor that you have never tasted before. Try it today and you will try it always. Arthur Kookman, sought by the police of Long Island for having blown up two churches and a nurses' home, was arrested today on a charge of filing a false income tax return. While being arraigned in court, he fired two shots at the judge, one of them killing Sergeant Jeremiah Kookberg in whose apartment police later found seventy-six shotguns, thirty-seven vacuum cleaners, forty-two washing machines, one hundred and fifty refrigerators, and three million dollars' worth of heroin. You will think you're in heaven when you taste Tiddly-Bits, the wonderful new chocolate-covered candy mints, as sweet as an angel's kiss."

My long Spooky Time session with the babble box in my living-room revealed still another source of what appears to me to be a desire, or compulsion, to drive the nation crazy. This is radio's apparently incurable addiction to frightening statistics. Many of these grow out of a basically worthy attempt to interest listeners in contributing money to various campaigns on behalf of research in heart disease, cancer, muscular dystrophy, and the like. Whoever writes most of these appeals seems invariably constrained to say something like this: "Every eleven seconds in America some man, woman, or child is stricken with Googleman's disease" or "There are more than eleven million people in the United States who suffer from unilateral mentalitis or allied ailments." Among the statistics that I gathered in the course of one afternoon were these consoling figures: there are nineteen million accidents every year in our nation; more than fourteen million Americans have, or have had, some serious mental derangement; fifty-two million dollars' worth of merchandise, comprising all forms of food, is stolen every year from American supermarkets.

It may be that radio, in flooding the daytime and nighttime air with horrible news and distressing statistics, banks on the well-established psychological truth that a person is not so much shocked by what happens to somebody else as relieved by the realization that he is, at least for the time being, unstricken and undead. The vast accumulation of all this twisted relief, however, is bound to take its toll of the American mass mind. One afternoon I was joined in front of my radio by three friends who had expressed doubt that so much hell and horror was calmly, or blithely, broadcast to the people of this jumpy republic. They ended up with the admission that I was by no means exaggerating, but even playing the situation down a bit. "Well," said one of them, with a heavy sigh, "*we* are still here." To which another replied, "As the fellow said at the Alamo."

There is, believe it or not, good news about the United States of America easily available to every radio press department if the gloomy gentlemen would care to look for it. Medical research, for instance, is continually turning up new devices and techniques for the cure, or alleviation, of almost all ailments. These are usually reported only in medical journals, but, alas, they do not have the impact of death, derangement, and disaster. I do not, of course, recommend sweetness and light or censorship, but merely the application of that now most uncommon of human qualities, common sense. The latest statistics that I have heard over the air, announced calmly by one school of reporters and gleefully by the other, asserted that a careful examination of some thousands of Americans proved that only eighteen percent of them were mentally well. Just think of it, folks—if there were a hundred guests at the New Year's Eve party you attended, only eighty-two of them were kooky, cuckoo, crazy, or nuts. Incidentally, the prevalent use of the word *disturbed* to take in all forms and degrees of mental aberration serves only to intensify the encircling gloom. For example, if one says, "She is disturbed by her husband's drinking," it implies that the wife has been driven crazy by it.

Not long ago a woman who was trapped in a New York subway fire, but managed to fight her way to safety, said, "It was wonderful to see people and light." An excellent combination, people and light. We ought to try to bring them together more often.

The Topaz Cufflinks Mystery

WHEN THE MOTORCYCLE COP came roaring up, unexpectedly, out of Never-Never Land (the way motorcycle cops do), the man was on his hands and knees in the long grass beside the road, barking like a dog. The woman was driving slowly along in a car that stopped about eighty feet away; its headlights shone on the man: middle-aged, bewildered, sedentary. He got to his feet.

"What's goin' on here?" asked the cop. The woman giggled. "Cock-eyed," thought the cop. He did not glance at her.

"I guess it's gone," said the man. "I—ah—could not find it."

"What was it?"

"What I lost?" the man squinted, unhappily. "Some—some cufflinks; topazes set in gold." He hesitated: the cop didn't seem to believe him. "They were the color of a fine Moselle," said the man. He put on a pair of spectacles which he had been holding in his hand. The woman giggled.

"Hunt things better with ya glasses off?" asked the cop. He pulled his motorcycle to the side of the road to let a car pass. "Better pull over off the concrete, lady," he said. She drove the car off the roadway.

"I'm nearsighted," said the man. "I can hunt things at a distance with my glasses on, but I do better with them off if I am

63

close to something." The cop kicked his heavy boots through the grass where the man had been crouching.

"He was barking," ventured the lady in the car, "so that I could see where he was." The cop pulled his machine up on its standard; he and the man walked over to the automobile.

"What I don't get," said the officer, "is how you lose ya cufflinks a hundred feet in front of where ya car is; a person usually stops his car *past* the place he loses somethin', not a hundred feet before he gits *to* the place."

The lady laughed again; her husband got slowly into the car, as if he were afraid the officer would stop him any moment. The officer studied them.

"Been to a party?" he asked. It was after midnight.

"We're not drunk, if that's what you mean," said the woman, smiling. The cop tapped his fingers on the door of the car.

"You people didn't lose no topazes," he said.

"Is it against the law for a man to be down on all fours beside a road, barking in a perfectly civil manner?" demanded the lady.

"No, ma'am," said the cop. He made no move to get on his motorcycle, however, and go on about his business. There was just the quiet chugging of the cycle engine and the auto engine, for a time.

"I'll tell you how it was, Officer," said the man, in a crisp, new tone. "We were settling a bet. O.K.?"

"O.K.," said the cop, "Who won?" There was another pulsing silence.

"The lady bet," said her husband, with dignity, as though he were explaining some important phase of industry to a newly hired clerk, "the lady bet that my eyes would shine like a cat's do at night, if she came upon me suddenly close to the ground alongside the road. We had passed a cat, whose eyes gleamed. We had passed several persons, whose eyes did *not* gleam—"

"Simply because they were above the light and not under it," said the lady. "A man's eyes would gleam like a cat's if people were ordinarily caught by headlights at the same angle as cats

are." The cop walked over to where he had left his motorcyle, picked it up, kicked the standard out, and wheeled it back.

"A cat's eyes," he said, "are different than yours and mine. Dogs, cats, skunks, it's all the same. They can see in a dark room."

"Not in a *totally* dark room," said the lady.

"Yes, they can," said the cop.

"No, they can't; not if there is no light at all in the room, not if it's absolutely *black*," said the lady. "The question came up the other night; there was a professor there and he said there must be at least a ray of light, no matter how faint."

"That may be," said the cop, after a solemn pause, pulling at his gloves. "But people's eyes don't shine—I go along these roads every night an' pass hunderds of cats and hunderds of people."

"The people are never close to the ground," said the lady.

"*I* was close to the ground," said her husband.

"Look at it this way," said the cop. "I've seen wildcats in *trees* at night, and *their* eyes shine."

"There you are!" said the lady's husband. "That proves it."

"I don't see how," said the lady. There was another silence.

"Because a wildcat in a tree's eyes are higher than the level of a man's," said her husband. The cop may possibly have followed this, the lady obviously did not, neither one said anything. The cop got on his machine, raced his engine, seemed to be thinking about something, and throttled down. He turned to the man.

"Took ya glasses off so the headlights wouldn't make ya glasses shine, huh?" he asked.

"That's right," said the man. The cop waved his hand, triumphantly, and roared away. "Smart guy," said the man to his wife, irritably.

"I still don't see where the wildcat proves anything," said his wife. He drove off slowly.

"Look," he said. "You claim that the whole thing depends on how *low a cat's* eyes are; I—"

"I didn't say that; I said it all depends on how *high a man's eyes* . . ."

Two O'Clock
at the Metropole

JUST A FEW MINUTES before two o'clock on the hot, sticky morning of Tuesday, July 16th, 1912, a man sauntered up to a table in the café of the old Hotel Metropole on Forty-third Street near Broadway and spoke to another man who sat there. "Somebody wants to see you outside, Herman," he said. In that casual sentence was spoken the doom of the famous and flourishing Hotel Metropole; it closed its doors not long afterward because of what happened in the next minute. The man at the table got up and walked briskly out onto the street, the other man following him. The one who had been addressed as Herman stood under the bright lights of the hotel's marquee, looking around for whoever it was wanted to see him. He didn't have to wait long. Four short dark men jumped out of a gray automobile standing at the curb, closed in on him, and fired six shots. That was the end of Herman Rosenthal, the gambler, and the beginning of one of the most celebrated murder cases in our history. Two days before this happened, Rosenthal had become known to the reading public. The *World* had printed an affidavit of his on that day charging that a police lieutenant named Charles Becker had exacted "protection money" from him and had then raided and closed his gambling house. It had also been intimated in the newspaper that Rosenthal would go before the grand jury and involve Becker even more deeply in corruption.

The murderers hadn't bothered to remove or obliterate the license plates of the gray touring car, because, as it transpired later, they had been told that "the cops are fixed" and nobody would do anything to them on account of their little job. But they reckoned without the *World*, District Attorney Charles S. Whitman, and a man named Charles Gallagher, a cabaret singer, who had just happened to be passing by. Gallagher caught the license number of the car: 41313 N.Y. He went immediately to the West Forty-seventh Street police station, reported the number, and was instantly thrown in jail for his pains. His information might have been completely ignored (the police had license numbers of their own to report, all of them wrong) had not a *World* reporter rung Whitman out of bed. The District Attorney got to the police station at three-twenty-five in the morning, learned about Gallagher, demanded his release, and got men to work on that license number. Before dawn the driver of the gray car, a man named Shapiro, was arrested in his bed in a room near Washington Square. Shapiro told Whitman his car had been hired that night by a man known as Billiard Ball Jack Rose.

Born Jacob Rosenzweig, in Poland, Jack Rose, thirty-five years old, was known in certain circles as the slickest poker player in town and as a graft collector for Lieutenant Becker, head of the Strong Arm Squad, which, among other things, "looked after" gambling joints in the city. There were hundreds of such places. A very popular one, on the second floor of a building at the northwest corner of Forty-second Street and Sixth Avenue, was run by a suave gentleman called Bridgie Webber. Rosenthal's place was nearby, at 104 West Forty-fifth Street. The Forties writhed with gambling joints running wide open. They all paid tribute to Charles Becker. His salary was only $2,200 a year, but it came out later that he had, in one nine-month period, banked almost $60,000. All his graft money was collected for him by Baldy Jack Rose (he had several nicknames). Becker lived in a mansion of a house he had built on Olinville Avenue in the Bronx. It still stands there; Judge

Peter Sheil lived in it until his death some years ago, and his widow died there last fall.

Two days after the assassination, Rose turned up at Police Headquarters, and the case's most unusual figure thus made his formal advent. Soft-spoken, a snappy dresser—his ties and shirts and socks always matched—Rose's physiognomy was not unlike that of Peter Lorre, in Lorre's more familiar make-up. Rose had not a hair on his head; even his eyebrows and eyelashes were gone, the result of typhoid in infancy. He admitted, lightly, that he had hired Shapiro's car; he had hired it to go uptown and visit a relative. He was put in a cell in the Tombs, where he was shortly joined by two other suspects, Bridgie Webber and another gambler named Harry Vallon. Webber had sent the widow Rosenthal $50 to help toward the funeral of Herman. All three men protested their innocence; they all had alibis.

The Rosenthal murder case bloomed blackly on the front pages of all the papers. Here was a more exciting story than even the story of the *Titanic*, which had sunk three months before. Various curious characters began to come into the case, enlivening it. There was a tough gangster chief named Big Jack Zelig (it was at this time that the word *gangster* was coined). There was a strange, blinking little man named Sam Schepps. One week after the murder, the harried Whitman, who was to become Governor because of his prosecution of this case, announced he would give immunity to anyone who named the "real culprit." Rose, Webber, and Vallon, all good poker players, knew when it was time to quit bluffing. They made prompt confessions. They charged that Lieutenant Becker had commissioned them to arrange the murder of Herman Rosenthal. They told who the actual killers were, the men for whom Rose had hired the car, and four unforgettable names were added to the annals of American crime: Lefty Louie, Gyp the Blood, Whitey Lewis, Dago Frank. We can dismiss briefly this infamous quartet, each of whom appears to have got $250, a big price at the time, for croaking Rosenthal. They were henchmen of the gang leader, Big Jack Zelig, who obeyed Becker but hated him. People were eager to hear a gangster chief testify, but they never got the chance; just as the case was about to come to trial Big Jack Zelig was found one day shot to death. So was the proprietor of a small café who had squealed on Dago Frank, the first of the four killers to be found and arrested. But Rose, Vallon, and Webber lived to testify; the District Attorney saw to it that they were carefully guarded. They lived in style in their cells. Lefty and Gyp and Whitey and the Dago were convicted in November, 1912, and speedily sentenced to death, although they weren't executed until a year and a half later. It was Becker, and not the four gunmen, who most interested the public—and Whitman. The case against the big, suave policeman was harder to prove.

Becker's first trial took place three months after the murder. Billiard Ball Jack Rose, neatly dressed in a dark blue suit, his shoes brightly shined, was the State's star witness. He told the jury that Becker had said to him, "Have Rosenthal murdered—cut his throat—dynamite him—anything!" Rose testified that Becker had advanced Rosenthal the money to open up his gambling house, had quarreled with him, and finally raided the place. Rosenthal, unable to interest Whitman at the time, had taken his plaint to the *World*. Things looked black for Becker, but the testimony of the three gamblers who had turned State's evidence was, under the law, not enough to convict. There had to be a corroborating witness, somebody entirely outside the crime. It was here that Sam Schepps, a cocky little man peering through spectacles, was brought forward by the State. Rose had told about a remarkable meeting, held in a vacant lot far uptown in Harlem and attended by himself, Vallon, Webber, and Becker, at which, Rose said, the police lieutenant had commanded them to get rid of Rosenthal. Schepps, a kind of hanger-on and toady of the gamblers, had witnessed this meeting, it was claimed, but at a distance. He swore he had had no idea what the four men were talking about; he had merely seen them talking together. On this extraordinary evidence about an extraordinary conference, Becker was sentenced to death. His lawyers appealed. Sixteen months went by, and then the Court of Appeals rejected the decision of the lower court, attacking the reliability of Schepps' testimony, declaring that he was obviously an accomplice of the three gamblers.

On the sixth of May, 1914, almost two years after Rosenthal's death, Becker went on trial again. At this trial a defense attorney turned on Rose and said, sharply, "When you were planning this murder, where was your conscience?" Rose answered, agonizedly but promptly, "My conscience was completely under the control of Becker." That seems to have been the truth about Baldy Jack Rose. Like many another gambler, and many a gangster, he lived in abject fear of the cold, overbearing, and ruthless police lieutenant. It was dangerous to cross Becker; he had railroaded dozens of men who had. Becker's lawyers claimed the gamblers had killed Rosenthal on their own, afraid of what he might reveal about them. Nobody much believed this. At this second trial— presided over by the youngish Samuel Seabury—a new corroborating witness was somehow found, a man named James Marshall, a vaudeville actor. He testified he had seen the gamblers and the lieutenant talking in the vacant lot on the night in question. His testimony was accepted; the defense failed to break it down. Becker was sentenced to death again, and this time the higher court did not interfere. He was executed, a maundering, broken hulk, on July 30th, 1915, a little more than three years after the slaying of Herman Rosenthal. Charles S. Whitman was then Governor of New York. He was considered criminally libelled by the inscription on a silver plate which Mrs. Becker had placed upon her husband's coffin. It read:

CHARLES BECKER
Murdered July 30, 1915
by
GOVERNOR WHITMAN

The plate was removed by order of Inspector Joseph Faurot, and the police lieutenant's widow replaced it with one bearing only his name and the dates of his birth and death. The *Lusitania* had been sunk two months earlier, and the memory of Becker was soon lost in the files of newspapers preoccupied with headlines of war.

Whitman, after retiring from politics, returned to the practice of law. He died of a heart attack in 1947, at the age of seventy-eight. Sam Schepps and Bridgie Webber died more than twenty years ago. What happened to James Marshall, the vaudeville actor, and to Charles Gallagher, the cabaret singer, it would be hard to find out. Webber, after the trials, went to live in New Jersey. He became, finally, vice president and secretary of the Garfield Paper Box Company of Passaic. He had lived in Fair Lawn, New Jersey, and worked in Passaic for twenty years as William Webber, a man without a past, until, in 1933, he appeared as a witness in a trial over there. A lawyer asked him on the stand if he was not the Bridgie Webber of the Rosenthal case. He admitted that he was. It seems to have made little difference to his friends and business associates. He died on the thirtieth of July, 1936. There may have been some, reading of his end, who found ironic significance in the fact that Charles Becker also died on the thirtieth of July, twenty-one years before.

Jack Rose did not withdraw from the view of men after the files of the Rosenthal-Becker case were closed. He preferred to be called simply Jack, and discouraged the use of the nicknames that had made him notorious, but he did not sulk in the shadows of life or attempt to disguise himself. He wore a cap to cover his baldness, but scorned the use of a toupee. He came boldly out into the open during the war years, and went from camp to camp lecturing soldiers on the evils of gambling and other vices. He lived in a fourteen-room house in a quiet suburban community with his wife and two sons, and when he wasn't lecturing on "Humanology," which he said meant the science of being human, he exhorted the children of his neighborhood to lead clean lives, and told them how he had ended up in reform school as a bad boy, where he first made contact with the underworld. He acquired a Chautauqua air, and the ardent platform manner of a reformer. His Humanology Motion Picture Corporation, founded in 1915, ended in failure two years later, but not until after he had produced six pictures based on the poems of his idol and friend, Ella Wheeler Wilcox. He liked to display a jewelled ring he wore, which Mrs. Wilcox had left him in her will. "She got the ring from an Indian rajah she met on this world tour," he said, proudly.

Jack Rose was an able and energetic businessman, and Humanology Pictures, more an expiation than an enterprise, was one of his few failures. Before he came to New York in the Becker regime, he had had a varied career in Connecticut. He ran a hotel in Bridgeport for a while, promoted prizefights in Hartford, managed the Danbury baseball team, and became part owner of the Norwich baseball team, gambling and playing the races on the side. Rose never had any trouble getting financial backing. His principal and most successful business venture after the trials was the establishment of a chain of roadside restaurants between Milford, Connecticut, and Lynbrook, Long Island. The restaurants were large and impressive and well run. "The largest one seats 248 persons and can serve 3,000 meals a day," he liked to boast. He supervised the planning of sunken gardens, and planned a twelve-piece orchestra for his favorite unit in the chain. Most of his customers didn't know who he was, and he was satisfied with that. He never brought up his past except in his talks to the soldiers and the children. If a reporter called on him, as one did occasionally for a Sunday feature story, he was not evasive, but answered questions directly. What he mostly wanted to talk about, though, was some new gadget he was installing, such as a hamburger machine, which he liked to show off to visitors. He rarely came to New York and, when he did, avoided his old haunts, and made his headquarters at the uptown millinery shop of a relative. If anybody recognized him and wanted to talk, he would talk. Billiard Ball Jack Rose's adjustment to life was never achieved by the manager of one of his restaurants, Harry Vallon. Vallon and his wife lived obscurely, refused to talk about themselves, and would hastily disappear if the subject came up. Once when Vallon dropped in on Jack at the main restaurant, he was introduced to a New York reporter. He turned on his heel without a word, hurried out to his car, and drove away.

Jack Rose died October 4, 1947, at the age of seventy-two, a few months after the death of Whitman. Nobody knows what became of Harry Vallon. The files of the *Times*, the *Herald Tribune*, and the Associated Press contain no mention of Vallon after the middle thirties. The Police Department has no record of him, either, since that time. If alive, he would be in his eighties, but it is likely that he died obscurely, possibly under an assumed name, where and when nobody may ever find out.

John's Chop House, which had occupied the site of Rosenthal's place at 104 West Forty-fifth Street, is no longer standing. The Sixth Avenue Urban Garage, Inc., completed on November 15, 1955, is located at 104 now. Nobody there ever heard about the notorious gambling house, or of the gambler who became one of the most celebrated figures in the annals of New York crime.

The Man Who Knew Too Little

THE MAN IN THE Café de Flore with the raincoat and the tired, worried look came over to our table. I had noticed him several times before, as one habitué of a café notices another. It was late and we had been there a long time. "May I sit down?" he asked, and I stood up and said, "Certainly." He sat down and I looked at him and my wife looked at me. "This is my wife," I said finally. He nodded. I asked him if he would have a drink and he said that he would have coffee. I ordered coffee for him and a couple more of those *quarts* of champagne so popular in Paris cafés now, for Marion and myself.

"I want to put a problem to you," the man said, after he got his coffee. "I have selected you to put this problem to because I have no friends in Paris. I have seen you several times and I have figured you as a man who would not belong to a secret organization."

"Why wouldn't he?" asked my wife.

The man did not smile as he said, "Your husband, Madam, is bewildered, perhaps, but not apprehensive. I have gathered that his considerable problems grow out of a magnification of the inconsiderable, and sometimes of the unreal."

My wife nodded, as if she followed all this. "That's right," she said.

I adjusted my tie. "I belong to a college fraternity," I said.

"I mean a secret *political* organization," our guest said. "The kind of organization I belong to. I belong to such an organization."

"What organization is it?" my wife asked.

"I don't know," said the man. "That's what I wanted to talk to you about. What I want is a fresh viewpoint, an outside viewpoint."

"Have some brandy," I said. The man nodded and I ordered brandy and two more V.P.'s, as they call those little quarter bottles of champagne. "Begin wherever you think you ought to," I said.

The man studied his coffee cup, twisting the cup around in the saucer. "Some months ago," he began, "some months ago I became a member of a secret organization. The way these things happen, I suppose, in Paris. A man accosted me in a café, as I am accosting you."

"My husband does not want to belong to a secret organization," said my wife. "He's too busy; he's too nervous, too."

The man waved this aside. "This man did not speak to me," he said. "He simply summoned me. I followed him outside. I followed him into the Metro and we got off at La Motte-Picquot station and I followed him to a basement room in a building in some street around there. There was a table in the room and about ten or fifteen men were sitting around it. They seemed like conspirators. There was something afoot."

"Frenchmen?" I asked.

"I don't know," said the man. "They spoke a language with which I am not familiar. It sounded to me as if it might have been made up, a code language or something. They spoke very low and very fast. The only word I really got sounded like 'Xingu' or 'window'; they kept repeating that. I have been to a great many of their meetings."

We had finished our drinks and I ordered brandy all around. "I've got to get out of this!" the man exclaimed suddenly. "But I don't know how." There was a long silence; we were all thinking.

"Why don't you lay low?" asked my wife. We both looked at her. "They always lay low," she said.

"Hide?" asked the man. "Disappear? They'd track me down. They might kill me. You can't get out of secret organizations that way."

"What do you say to them? What do they say to you?" I asked.

"They never say anything to me and I never say anything, either," he said. "They don't seem to notice me—even when they deal the cards. I'm just there. No matter where I am on meeting nights, some man comes and summons me. Once he was in my room when I got back to my hotel. He just beckons."

"Are you an American?" my wife asked.

He just said, "I have lived in Paris a great many years."

"How about brandy?" I asked. We all had more brandy.

"Couldn't you just refuse to follow this man?" I asked.

"Oh," he said, "I'm past that point. I can't do that now. You Middle Westerners—you are from the Middle West, aren't you?—are always for beginning all over again."

"They'd kill him," my wife said to me, "because he knows too much."

"All he knows," I said, "is Xingu or window. That isn't too much."

The man was toying with a cufflink; he looked very worried. "I've got to get out of this," he said.

"Can't you make out whether they're trying to get somebody, or overthrow something, or what?" I said.

He shrugged. "They deal out cards once in a while," he said. "Each of us gets a card. You know what that means, in stories about such things, in fiction of the sort."

"If you get the ace of spades you have to kill somebody. Or sometimes you have to kill yourself," said my wife. "A brother officer leaves a gun in the room and goes away."

"Nonsense," I said.

"Nonsense," said my wife. "You listen to *us*. Why don't you ask them in Frenglish what it's all about?" Her eyes opened wide and bright as she said this. "Maybe they speak Frenglish," she said.

"You must try to let me tell the story," said the man patiently. "It is hard to know what anybody in Paris who meets in secret with anybody else is up to. Since General de Miller disappeared and then General Skoblin, the police have made discoveries which connect practically everybody with practically everybody else. They have seized papers in the apartment of a Russian named Bogovond in the rue de la Pompe which are said to show a relationship between the kidnapping of the two generals, the theft of the documents from Leon Trotsky, the suicide of Ivar Kreuger, the Stavisky affair, the slaying of Dmitri Novachin, and the murder of the secret agent Reiss in Switzerland. God knows what else. I may be mixed up in all that."

My wife leaned forward. "I know a man," she said, "who was suspected of being a spy for a country he can never remember. You tell them at the next meeting that you are not cut out for whatever it is. Tell them they're getting the wrong class of people."

"Look," I said, trying to bring it all back to some simple statement, "they must know you haven't understood a word. They must know you don't know too much. It's some monstrous mistake, it's some monstrous deception. Simply refuse to follow the man next time. Say '*Non compris*' to him, say 'Don't understand.'"

"Get policemen, too," said my wife.

The man in the raincoat sighed. "It's always this way," he said, "whenever I put the problem up to anybody." He finished his brandy and stood up. "Nobody has a way out."

I stood up too. "I'm sorry," I said. "But it isn't so easy, you know, offhand. Maybe if you gave us a little time."

"Some other time, maybe," said Marion.

The man put out his hand. "You will never see me again," he said. "I have troubled you enough. Pray forget about this. I thank you for your tolerance and for the coffee and the brandy." He walked over to the door and walked out.

I was surprised a few minutes later when he came back into the café and walked over to us again. I was paying the bill and my wife was leaning under the table hunting for a glove.

"I not only don't know what they talk about," he said. "I also, I forgot to say, do not know who the men are. I mean I couldn't identify any of them."

"Are they masked?" I asked.

"No, it isn't that," he said, "it isn't that. You see, *they are never the same crowd of men.*"

He walked over to the door and went out again into the night. I saw him turn up the collar of his raincoat and pull down his hat. It was raining, I figured.

My wife came up from under the table with the dusty glove. "What did the man want?" she asked.

"I don't know," I said. "Maybe I don't speak any known language, or something."

"I like people that speak known languages," said Marion. "All *my* family speak known languages." She had the look that means she wants an argument. It was too late for that; it was terribly late. We went back to the hotel, but not in the rain. It wasn't raining.

The Case Book of James Thurber

THE CASE OF the Gloucester Sympathizer was an easy one to crack, once I had sense enough to stop trying to crack it the hard way. I first heard about the Sympathizer one day last summer from a friend of mine at Annisquam, Massachusetts, near Gloucester. He told me he had called the Gloucester Telephone Company one day, to complain about something, and the operator had said, "One moment, please. I'll connect you with the Sympathizer." "She must have said 'supervisor,'" I said. This annoyed him, since he is proud of his ear and accuracy. "Not at all!" he snapped. "I said, 'Connect me with whom?' and she repeated, 'With the Sympathizer.'"

I wanted to know what the Sympathizer was like, when he finally connected with her. "Did she begin by saying, 'Heavens to Betsy, isn't that too bad! I'm dreadfully sorry.'" He looked disappointed. "She was courteous, crisp, and competent," he said. I reached for my hypodermic needle. "Was she terribly solicitous?" I demanded. He frowned. "No," he said, "she wasn't."

When I got back to my home in Cornwall, Connecticut, I picked up the phone and asked the Cornwall telephone operator to connect me with the Sympathizer. "You're a caution, Mr. Thurber," she said, laughed, and hung up. Then I called the long-distance operator in Torrington, fifteen miles away. She said there wasn't any Sympathizer in Torrington, but she was sorry it had happened, whatever it was. I could tell that she thought I was a caution, too. I was about to try Hartford, to see if there was a Sympathizer there, when it occurred to me to write the Gloucester Telephone Company and ask them about their Sympathizer. I got a prompt and cordial letter from the company, announcing that there wasn't any Sympathizer, and offering its consolations and best wishes. I got my violin out of its case and began sawing moodily in the general direction of "Chloe," lost in meditation. Naturally, I deduced at last, no reputable firm or corporation would employ a sympathizer, because the very existence of such a person would lend a note of gloom and insecurity to merchandising and other business transactions. I telephoned my friend and gave him the results of my findings in one sentence. "There isn't any Sympathizer," I told him. "Yes, there is," he snarled. "Go to hell," I said, and hung up.

The Case of the Gloucester Sympathizer was similar to the Case of the Young Woman Named Sherlock Holmes, a problem I solved the easy way a couple of years ago. George Spencer had told me that a guy he knew named Harry Huff was going to marry a girl named Sherlock Holmes. I said this was nonsense, because there isn't any girl named Sherlock Holmes. He said I didn't know anything about it. I said it was dangerous to believe everything one heard, and to go around repeating it. He snapped the leash back on his dog's collar, picked up its throwing stick, and went away.

I got out the phone book. There were two Henry Huffs listed, and I called the first one. "Nah," he said, "I'm living in sin with Dr. Watson. I thought everybody knew that." He was obviously the wrong Henry Huff, and I hung up on him. The second one turned out to be the right one. I asked him to spell out the name of his fiancée. Without hesitation, he said he didn't want to, so I mentioned George Spencer and what he had said about Sherlock Holmes. Huff was annoyed, but he finally told me the name of the girl he was going to marry, one Shirley Combs.

It reminded me of the Curious Adventure of the Oral Surgeons' Mouse, which had taken place thirty years ago when I was a reporter. The city editor answered the phone one day, and then sent for me. "The oral surgeons in convention here are about to operate on a mouse," he said. "Slide over and watch it." I went away and came right back. "What's the matter?" snarled the editor. "Wouldn't the mouse open wide?" "It wasn't a mouse," I snarled. "It was a mouth, it was a guy's mouth." This was a great blow to the editor, almost as great as that which befell the little boy in Pennsylvania Station who thought the announcer was announcing the Make Believe Train, only to find out it was just the old Maple Leaf Express, on its routine way again.

The Anatomy of Confusion is a large subject, and I have no intention of writing the standard treatise on it, but I offer to whoever does, the most singular of all my cases, the Case of the Cockeyed Spaniard. This remarkable piece of confusion took place in Columbus, Ohio, as long ago as 1922. I lived next door to a young couple named Dan and Janet Henderson at the time. Dan was a well-known reveller of the neighborhood, given to odd companions and peculiar pranks. One afternoon about six o'clock, Janet phoned me and asked me to come over. Her voice sounded wavy and troubled. "What's Dan up to now?" I asked. She sighed. "He's bringing home a cockeyed Spaniard," she said, "and I simply won't face them both alone." I slipped my brass knuckles into my pocket and went over to the Henderson house. "The only Spaniards I know of in Columbus," I told Janet, "are a dozen students at Ohio State, but I doubt that they would be cockeyed as early as six o'clock."

It transpired that Dan Henderson had phoned his ominous message while Mrs. Henderson was in the bath tub. Their colored maid Mary had answered the phone. I interviewed Mary in the kitchen. She was pop-eyed and nervous. The physical stature of the Spaniard and the degree of his intoxication had obviously become magnified in her mind. "I ain't goin' to mess around with no cockeyed Spaniard," she told me flatly. "If he mislests me, I'll hit him with a bottle." While we waited for Dan and his friend to show up, I began to apply my special methods to the case, and before long I had figured it out. No doubt you have, too, since you are probably smarter than I was in 1922.

When Dan came home to his frantic wife, he was carrying the cockeyed Spaniard in his arms, but the fellow was, of course, neither cockeyed nor Spanish. He was sad-eyed, four months old, sleepy, hungry, and definitely sober, as cute a cocker spaniel as you would ever want to see. Mary stubbornly clung to the name she had got over the phone, and her insistence on this pleasant distortion became generally known about town. People would call up the Henderson house and ask for her and say, "This is the Canine Census Bureau. What kind of dog do you have in your home?" Mary would always reply promptly and brightly, "He's a cockeyed Spaniard." I often wonder what ever became of her. I hope she is well and happy.

Mr. Preble Gets Rid of His Wife

M R. PREBLE was a plump middle-aged lawyer in Scarsdale. He used to kid with his stenographer about running away with him. "Let's run away together," he would say, during a pause in dictation. "All righty," she would say.

One rainy Monday afternoon, Mr. Preble was more serious about it than usual.

"Let's run away together," said Mr. Preble.

"All righty," said his stenographer. Mr. Preble jingled the keys in his pocket and looked out the window.

"My wife would be glad to get rid of me," he said.

"Would she give you a divorce?" asked the stenographer.

"I don't suppose so," he said. The stenographer laughed.

"You'd have to get rid of your wife," she said.

Mr. Preble was unusually silent at dinner that night. About half an hour after coffee, he spoke without looking up from his paper.

"Let's go down in the cellar," Mr. Preble said to his wife.

"What for?" she said, not looking up from her book.

"Oh, I don't know," he said. "We never go down in the cellar any more. The way we used to."

"We never did go down in the cellar that I remember," said Mrs. Preble. "I could rest easy the balance of my life if I never

84

went down in the cellar." Mr. Preble was silent for several minutes.

"Supposing I said it meant a whole lot to me," began Mr. Preble.

"What's come over you?" his wife demanded. "It's cold down there and there is absolutely nothing to do."

"We could pick up pieces of coal," said Mr. Preble. "We might get up some kind of a game with pieces of coal."

"I don't want to," said his wife. "Anyway, I'm reading."

"Listen," said Mr. Preble, rising and walking up and down. "Why won't you come down in the cellar? You can read down there, as far as that goes."

"There isn't a good enough light down there," she said, "and anyway, I'm not going to go in the cellar. You may as well make up your mind to that."

"Gee whiz!" said Mr. Preble, kicking at the edge of a rug. "Other people's wives go down in the cellar. Why is it you never want to do anything? I come home worn out from the office and you won't even go down in the cellar with me. God knows it isn't very far—it isn't as if I was asking you to go to the movies or someplace."

"I don't want to *go!*" shouted Mrs. Preble. Mr. Preble sat down on the edge of a davenport.

"All right, all *right*," he said. He picked up the newspaper again. "I wish you'd let me tell you more about it. It's—kind of a surprise."

"Will you quit harping on that subject?" asked Mrs. Preble.

"Listen," said Mr. Preble, leaping to his feet. "I might as well tell you the truth instead of beating around the bush. I want to get rid of you so I can marry my stenographer. Is there anything especially wrong about that? People do it every day. Love is something you can't control—"

"We've been all over that," said Mrs. Preble. "I'm not going to go all over that again."

"I just wanted you to know how things are," said Mr. Preble. "But you have to take everything so literally. Good Lord, do you

suppose I really wanted to go down in the cellar and make up some silly game with pieces of coal?"

"I never believed that for a minute," said Mrs. Preble. "I knew all along you wanted to get me down there and bury me."

"You can say that now—after I told you," said Mr. Preble. "But it would never have occurred to you if I hadn't."

"You didn't tell me; I got it out of you," said Mrs. Preble. "Anyway, I'm always two steps ahead of what you're thinking."

"You're never within a mile of what I'm thinking," said Mr. Preble.

"Is that so? I knew you wanted to bury me the minute you set foot in this house tonight." Mrs. Preble held him with a glare.

"Now that's just plain damn exaggeration," said Mr. Preble, considerably annoyed. "You knew nothing of the sort. As a matter of fact, I never thought of it till just a few minutes ago."

"It was in the back of your mind," said Mrs. Preble. "I suppose this filing woman put you up to it."

"You needn't get sarcastic," said Mr. Preble. "I have plenty of people to file without having her file. She doesn't know anything about this. She isn't in on it. I was going to tell her you had gone to visit some friends and fell over a cliff. She wants me to get a divorce."

"That's a laugh," said Mrs. Preble. "*That's* a laugh. You may bury me, but you'll never get a divorce."

"She knows that! I told her that," said Mr. Preble. "I mean—I told her I'd never get a divorce."

"Oh, you probably told her about burying me, too," said Mrs. Preble.

"That's not true," said Mr. Preble, with dignity. "That's between you and me. I was never going to tell a soul."

"You'd blab it to the whole world; don't tell me," said Mrs. Preble. "I know you." Mr. Preble puffed at his cigar.

"I wish you were buried now and it was all over with," he said.

"Don't you suppose you would get caught, you crazy thing?" she said. "They always get caught. Why don't you go to bed? You're just getting yourself all worked up over nothing."

"I'm not going to bed," said Mr. Preble. "I'm going to bury you in the cellar. I've got my mind made up to it. I don't know how I could make it any plainer."

"Listen," cried Mrs. Preble, throwing her book down, "will you be satisfied and shut up if I go down in the cellar? Can I have a little peace if I go down in the cellar? Will you let me alone then?"

"Yes," said Mr. Preble. "But you spoil it by taking that attitude."

"Sure, sure, I always spoil everything. I stop reading right in the middle of a chapter. I'll never know how the story comes out—but that's nothing to you."

"Did I make you start reading the book?" asked Mr. Preble. He opened the cellar door. "Here, you go first."

"Brrr," said Mrs. Preble, starting down the steps. "It's *cold* down here! You *would* think of this, at this time of year! Any other husband would have buried his wife in the summer."

"You can't arrange those things just whenever you want to," said Mr. Preble. "I didn't fall in love with this girl till late fall."

"Anybody else would have fallen in love with her long before that. She's been around for years. Why is it you always let other men get in ahead of you? Mercy, but it's dirty down here! What have you got there?"

"I was going to hit you over the head with this shovel," said Mr. Preble.

"You were, huh?" said Mrs. Preble. "Well, get that out of your mind. Do you want to leave a great big clue right here in the middle of everything where the first detective that comes snooping around will find it? Go out in the street and find some piece of iron or something—something that doesn't belong to you."

"Oh, all right," said Mr. Preble. "But there won't be any piece of iron in the street. Women always expect to pick up a piece of iron anywhere."

"If you look in the right place you'll find it," said Mrs. Preble. "And don't be gone long. Don't you dare stop in at the cigarstore. I'm not going to stand down here in this cold cellar all night and freeze."

"All right," said Mr. Preble. "I'll hurry."

"And shut that *door* behind you!" she screamed after him. "Where were you born—in a barn?"

The Trial of
the Old Watchdog

A N OLD experienced collie, who had been a faithful country watchdog for many years, was arrested one summer's day and accused of the first-degree murder of a lamb. Actually, the lamb had been slain by a notorious red fox who had planted the still-warm body of his victim in the collie's kennel.

The trial was held in a kangaroo court presided over by Judge Wallaby. The jury consisted of foxes, and all the spectators were foxes. A fox named Reynard was prosecuting attorney. "Morning, Judge," he said.

"God bless you, boy, and good luck," replied Judge Wallaby jovially.

A poodle named Beau, an old friend and neighbor of the collie, represented the accused watchdog. "Good morning, Judge," said the poodle.

"Now I don't want you to be too clever," the Judge warned him. "Cleverness should be confined to the weaker side. That's only fair."

A blind woodchuck was the first creature to take the stand, and she testified that she saw the collie kill the lamb.

"The witness is blind!" protested the poodle.

"No personalities, please," said the Judge severely. "Perhaps the witness saw the murder in a dream or a vision. This would give her testimony the authority of revelation."

"I wish to call a character witness," said the poodle.

"We have no character witnesses," said Reynard smoothly, "but we have some charming character assassins."

One of these, a fox named Burrows, was called to the stand. "I didn't actually see this lamb killer kill this lamb," said Burrows, "but I almost did."

"That's close enough," said Judge Wallaby.

"Objection," barked the poodle.

"Objection overruled," said the Judge. "It's getting late. Has the jury reached a verdict?"

The forefox of the jury stood up. "We find the defendant guilty," he said, "but we think it would be better to acquit him, nonetheless. If we hang the defendant, his punishment will be over. But if we acquit him of such dark crimes as murder, concealing the body, and associating with poodles and defense attorneys, nobody will ever trust him again, and he will be suspect all the days of his life. Hanging is too good for him, and much too quick."

"Guilt by exoneration!" Reynard cried. "What a lovely way to end his usefulness!"

And so the case was dismissed and court was adjourned, and everybody went home to tell about it.

Moral: Thou shalt not blindfold justice by pulling the wool over her eyes.

The Secret Life
of Harold Winney

HAROLD WINNEY, who seemed to me, and still does, unreal as the look and sound of his name, was Ross's private secretary from 1935 until the middle of August, 1941. In his years with Ross, the pallid, silent young man steadily swindled the editor out of a total of seventy-one thousand dollars. His multiple forgeries, his raids and inroads upon Ross's bank account, expense account, salary, and securities, belong in McKelway's *Of Crime and Rascality*, somewhere between the magnificently complicated defalcations of the Wily Wilby and the fantastic dollar bill counterfeiting of Old 880. Bankers, tax men, and accountants still shake their heads in wonder and disbelief over the case history of Harold Winney, which has become a part of the folklore and curiosa of American capitalism.

Nobody at the *New Yorker* offices knew, or cared, very much about Harold Winney, who had been born about 1910 in or near Albany, New York, the only child of a man who died when his son was very young, and of a mother who fortunately did not live long enough to know about her son's crimes. I remember Winney mainly for his cold small voice, his pale nimble fingers, and his way of moving about the corridors and offices like a shadow. I do not believe that Harold Ross ever looked at the man closely enough to have been able to describe him accurately. He was

91

what Ross once irritably described as a "worm"—that is, an unimportant cog in the *New Yorker* wheel, a noncreative person. As a secretary, Winney was competent and quiet.

He took dictation speedily, and transcribed his notes the same way. I would be sitting in my office, and suddenly his voice would surprise me, for I never heard him enter the room. "Mr. Ross would like your opinion on this," he would say, and hand me a typewritten query about something or other; this was in the days when I could see to read. He would stand there absolutely motionless, without a word, and wait for me to tell him what I thought, or to type my reply on a piece of paper; then he would silently vanish. He was master of the art of protective immobility. I remember that he was neat to the point of being immaculate, but the clothes he wore were as unobtrusive as his manner. When investigators examined his apartment, they found, among other things, a hundred and three suits of clothes which he had bought with the money stolen from Ross. They also found, in a private correspondence file, a long exchange of letters with a real estate firm in Tahiti. Winney had planned, a little vaguely, to flee when he had piled up enough of his employer's money, but the embezzler never does get enough, and when, in the summer of 1941, his crimes were discovered, the war was on and he could not obtain a passport.

Discovery, in the end, was inevitable. The miracle is that it didn't come years sooner. If Winney drank or smoked, it was usually in moderation, and there was only one subject in the world that could light up his cold eyes and his impassive face. That was horse racing. He was a horse player, completely addicted to it, and a steady loser. Nobody will ever know how much he lost in gambling on the horses, or what exactly became of the seventy-one thousand dollars he stole. Copies of his private letters to men friends revealed that he spent his money lavishly upon some of them, buying one an expensive sports car, outfitting another with complete skiing equipment, and giving them money for their vacations and holidays. Investigators were baffled at every turn in trying to trace what happened to Ross's money. There was,

however, a record of a big champagne party Winney gave in a suite at the Astor Hotel on the night in November, 1940, when Roosevelt was elected President for the third time. "I walked past the Astor several times that night with friends," Ross told me gloomily, "and I guess I was hit on the head by my own champagne corks." He gestured toward the room just outside his own office where Winney had had his desk and typewriter. "He sat out there and fed me cake," Ross moaned.

Winney was, by a familiar caprice of nature, incapable of emotional interest in females, and this was as apparent to all of us, except Ross, as the simple fact that Mary Pickford is a woman. To Ross, however, who never scrutinized his secretary or gave him any real thought, he was nothing more than a chair in his office or the ash tray on his desk. "Did you know he was *that* kind of a man?" Ross asked me and the rest of us, and we all just stared at him and said, "Yes, didn't you?" Ross would brush this aside and say, "Then it explains the whole business. That kind of guy always wants to ruin the normal man."

Ross was by no means, of course, financially ruined by Winney, for he still had plenty of money of his own after the loss of the seventy-one thousand dollars.

During the almost seven years that Winney robbed Ross, day after day, the editor was at the peak of his work and his worries in every field. In 1935, the year Winney came to work for him, Ross's daughter was born, and the magazine was developing rapidly in every way. In the midst of all this, Ross recognized the necessity of "delegating" some of his duties and some of his worries. He made the big mistake of delegating to Harold Winney complete control, without any safeguard whatever, of his bank accounts and securities—he had two separate accounts in one bank. The bank tellers and vice-presidents became familiar with the quiet, well-behaved, efficient young man who was Ross's private secretary, and in whom, the editor had made it clear, he reposed every trust. Thus, when Winney showed up at the teller's cage with a check made out to cash, signed with the unmistakable signature of H. W. Ross, the check was not subjected to more than casual scrutiny. Even if it had been, Winney's forgery of Ross's name was so perfect that after the secretary's death, the few canceled checks that could be found baffled not only handwriting experts but even Ross himself, who could not swear whether a given signature was his own or Winney's. Winney's own initials were H. W. and all he had to imitate were the six letters of H. W. Ross. He became an expert at it.

As the years went on, he grew bolder and bolder, and in one week, the record shows, cashed three separate checks for a total of six thousand dollars. At that period, Ross's main financial interest was in his friend Dave Chasen's restaurant in Hollywood. About the time that Harold Winney began robbing Ross, the restaurant began to make money. Ross had originally lent Chasen three thousand dollars, a generous personal loan of the kind for which he was well known to his intimates. Sums of money like that did not bother Ross when it came to helping out one of the men to whom he was most devoted. Later he began investing in the restaurant and his profits increased, but he could never quite accommodate himself to the idea that he deserved the profits, which amounted finally to more than two hundred thousand dollars. "Goddam it, I never intended to make a lot of money out of Dave's place," he once told a lawyer. "It's hard for me to think he owes me anything, except on the basis of personal loans." The difference between a loan and an investment had to be explained to him patiently. "I know, I know all that," he would say, putting on his well-known expression of worry and wonder.

Winney began cautiously by forging six checks in 1935 for a total of about fourteen hundred dollars; the next year he forged seven checks for a total of nineteen hundred dollars. In 1937 there were nine checks, and the amount was twenty-nine hundred dollars, and in 1938, the year before he threw caution to the winds, he forged seven checks for twenty-seven hundred and thirty dollars. During all this time he was careful to fill out checkbook stubs and reconcile them precisely with Ross's monthly bank statements. He had soon discovered, but probably couldn't believe it, that Ross did not want to be bothered by studying his checkbooks or monthly statements. So Winney "summarized" them, as he explained it to Ross, and would simply lay a typed sheet of paper on Ross's desk when he was asked about the state of his account. If Ross spotted some familiar amount, such as $113.13, and said, "I thought that check went through last month," Winney would simply tell him quietly that he was wrong. The cake became easier and easier to feed to Ross, and Winney finally abandoned entirely the unnecessary work of justification. He would simply tear a check out of a checkbook, fill it out for whatever amount he wanted, sign Ross's name, and cash it at the bank. When he really began to splurge with Ross's money and visit the bank several times a week, he would hand in the check and wink slyly at the teller, as if to say, "The old boy's at it again." I don't know how many persons, outside the *New Yorker* and Ross's circle of friends, knew how often Ross gambled and how often he lost, but it was scarcely a state secret. Dozens of checks for gambling losses, averaging around five hundred dollars, were duplicated by Winney before he sent them, with Ross's genuine signature on them, to the lucky winners. During 1939 and 1940 and up until the end of July, 1941, Winney forged a hundred and sixty checks for a total of about sixty-two thousand dollars. By the end of July, 1941, he had withdrawn all of his employer's salary through December and, along with it, several thousand dollars of Ross's expense account money.

Winney was a well-implemented student of his employer. He was, however, at all times skating on ice that grew thinner and thinner, and he must have known that sooner or later it would break under him. It may be that he hoped to restore the money he had taken if he could only win a large amount on the horses or make some quick and profitable investment, but nobody knows about that, or if anybody does, nothing has ever been revealed. Winney's friends, or such of them as were found and talked to, claimed they knew nothing about his secret life, and this may well have been true. He was as tight-mouthed as he was thin-lipped.

The withdrawal in advance of Ross's salary and expense account money had to be accomplished through the *New Yorker's* own business department, and, in spite of the tension between the editor and that department, it remained something of a miracle that nothing was said to Ross about these massive withdrawals until the middle of August, 1941. One man in the business department, who has been there for more than thirty years, told me what I already knew: that if the business department ever mentioned money to Ross, he yelled them down, or said they were crazy, or announced that he didn't want to talk about it and hung up the phone. There were years during which he would refuse to discuss anything at all with Fleischmann, and such communications as passed between them were carried on circuitously. Winney was also a close student of this situation.

In 1938 Ross and his second wife spent several months in France and England, and before he left he put his securities in Winney's hands, giving him power of attorney over them. In order to replenish this or that account, in a crisis, the secretary would sell some of Ross's securities. Ross both played into Winney's hands and made things a bit difficult for him by carrying loose checks in his pocket and making them out to this person or that or to this firm or that, sometimes remembering to tell Winney about them the next day, but often forgetting it. In this way,

Winney could never be sure what situation would confront him at the end of any given month.

During the last year of Winney's peculations, he caused Ross to be overdrawn multiple times at the bank. When this situation occurred, Winney would either transfer some funds from the account in Jane Grant's name to Ross's own account, or cover up by selling some more of Ross's securities. The "mad, intelligent Ross," as Janet Flanner once called him, had simply forgotten to cancel Winney's power of attorney, after the editor got back from France. Ross expected to get loyalty from those around him the way he expected to get his mail, but he didn't always get that, either. All communications from the bank and several letters from a firm of tax experts, suggesting that they supervise Ross's financial interests, were simply torn up and thrown away by Ross's secretary.

When it comes to money, bank accounts, and everything else fiscal or financial, I am not one to throw stones, but a pot as black as the kettle. I once had a checking account in a famous old Fifth Avenue bank, through the recommendation of Ralph Ingersoll, but after I had been overdrawn three times, I was invited to talk it over with a vice-president of the bank. He was shocked almost beyond words when he discovered that I did not fill out my checkbook stubs. "Then how do you know how much money you have in the bank?" he asked me, and I told him, "I estimate it." He turned a little white and his hand trembled. "You—*estimate* it?" he croaked. That bank was glad to get rid of me.

I have always had the good sense to let my wife handle my finances, but Ross would just have goggled at anyone who suggested that he put such a responsibility upon his own spouse. It was not only his strangeness about dough, but his erratic judgments of men, that put such a powerful temptation in the way of Harold Winney. One of those around him in the early years, a man he both liked and trusted, and rightly so, was Ralph Paladino. When he was young and single, Ralph took a course in public accounting at a night school, and Ross attended his graduation exercises. Ralph, it seemed to us in those days, kept track of everything for Ross. He was an expert on order, organization, dough, records, and everything else that Ross worried about. Then Ralph was married and after a while had children, and needed an increase of salary, and Ross would not okay this. I still get mad at him when I think about it, and I once bawled him out for it, after Ralph quit and took a better-paying job. "I haven't got time for little people," Ross snarled, and I told him that was a hell of a thing to say. He later apologized for it, murmured something about all the physical troubles that he had at the time, a jaw infection, his ulcers, and the spreading of the metatarsal bones of one foot. Ralph Paladino, by the way, is now head of the make-up department at *Newsweek*. Last year a man who works there told me, "He is our one most indispensable man."

Harold Ross had a lot of things to think about in 1941, including his approaching third marriage, three of my five eye operations, the war and all that it did to him, and a hundred other concerns. He himself had withdrawn some of his salary and expense account that year, and this gave Winney the idea of withdrawing the rest of it. Such transactions as this had to be okayed by the Miracle Man—during most of this period it was Ik Shuman. One day after Winney had withdrawn Ross's salary and expense money for October, November, and December, Raoul Fleischmann sent for Shuman and said, "Did you know that Ross is hard up?" They discussed the matter, and Ik said he would look into it.

For a while Ross simply did not believe, or even listen to, what Shuman had to tell him about his withdrawn salary. Then he sent for Winney. That doomed young man knew that he had come to the end of the line, but he didn't turn white, or begin shaking, or break down and confess. He simply double-talked Ross into deeper and deeper confusion, until the editor said, "Oh, the hell with it—I'll stop in at the bank tomorrow and find out all about it myself." That sentence was Harold Winney's death sentence. After work he went home to his expensive and tidily furnished apartment in Brooklyn, turned on the gas in the kitchen and took his own life.

When the body of Harold Winney was discovered the next day in his Brooklyn apartment, Ross was greatly upset, and when the first batch of his manifold forgeries came to light, he expressed pity for him, and even compassion, according to Shuman and Gene Kinkead, Ross's great "gumshoe." Kinkead had been assigned to find out as much as he could about what Winney had done to Ross, and when the staggering total of the quiet man's thefts became clear, Ross no longer said, as he had been saying, "The poor little guy." What mainly bothered Ross, however, was not the amount of his losses, but the feeling that his "friends at '21,'" as Shuman put it, would never get over kidding him about it all. So the actual total of the forgeries was not given out to the papers. They were told that it was somewhere between seventeen thousand and twenty thousand dollars. That's what Ross told me, too. I think that he was wrong about this. Any American can be taken for seventeen thousand or twenty thousand dollars, but it takes a really great eccentric to be robbed of seventy-one thousand dollars right under his busy nose.

I am told that Ross could not be reimbursed by the bank for his losses, because he had made this legally impossible by the way he ignored his monthly statements, and by his giving power of attorney to Winney, which he never withdrew. It seems that Ross did get five thousand dollars of Harold Winney's insurance money. What I remember mainly about the wreckage of that tragic August was a strange threat Ross made. He was going to get even with the bank, he said, by "hiring Steve Hannagan." Just what he expected that late, famous public relations man, sometimes known as the "Discoverer of Florida," to do, I have no way of knowing. Ross soon realized, of course, that publicity was precisely what he did not want.

Among those to whom Ross occasionally lost money at backgammon or gin rummy was a well-known New York publisher, and whenever he won from two hundred dollars to five hundred dollars from Ross, Winney would duplicate the check, so that Ross really always lost twice as much as he believed he had. Losing anything to a publisher was, to H. W. Ross, something that there could be nothing more deplorable than. He fought publishers, on behalf of writers, all his life, and wrote literally hundreds of letters bawling them out. One of these, to Marshall Best, runs to two thousand words. In a letter to Ross, the publisher had accused him of obscurantism, and Ross ended his reply, "Whee! Let's have oceans of obscurantism." Ross and the *New Yorker* never took any subsidiary rights at all from writers and artists, but were satisfied with first serial rights. When Ross found out that publishers often got a percentage of their authors' sales of movie or theater rights, he banged away at them on his trusty typewriter, and you could hear it all the way down the hall. He also fought them for better royalties for writers and for a more equable arrangement on anthologies. He once got a letter from Christopher La Farge, then president of the Authors' League, thanking him, on behalf of the authors of the country, for what he had been doing and was still doing.

I don't know how to end this account of the short, unhappy life of Harold Winney, but I guess I'll just put down what two different admirers of Ross, who did not know the Winney story, said, in the same voice, after I had told the tale. "What a wonderful man!" said one of them. "What a crazy guy!" said the other.

The Raven
by Edgar Allan Poe

ONCE UPON A MIDNIGHT DREARY, while I pondered, weak and
   weary,
Over many a quaint and curious volume of forgotten lore,—
While I nodded, nearly napping, suddenly there came a tapping,
As of someone gently rapping, rapping at my chamber door.
"'Tis some visitor," I muttered, "tapping at my chamber door;
        Only this, and nothing more."

Presently my soul grew stronger; hesitating then no longer,
"Sir," said I, "or madam, truly your forgiveness I implore;
But the fact is, I was napping, and so gently you came rapping,
And so faintly you came tapping, tapping at my chamber door,
That I scarce was sure I heard you."—Here I opened wide the
    door;
            Darkness there, and nothing more.

Open then I flung the shutter, when, with many a flirt and flutter,
In there stepped a stately raven of the saintly days of yore.
Not the least obeisance made he; not an instant stopped or stayed
  he;
But, with mien of lord or lady, perched above my chamber
  door,—
Perched above a bust of Pallas, just above my chamber door,—
    Perched, and sat, and nothing more.

"Prophet!" said I, "thing of evil!—prophet still, if bird or devil!
By that heaven that bends above us,—by that God we both adore,
Tell this soul with sorrow laden, if, within the distant Aidenn,
It shall clasp a sainted maiden, whom the angels name Lenore,
Clasp a fair and radiant maiden, whom the angels name Lenore!"
   Quoth the raven, "Nevermore!"

"Be that word our sign of parting, bird or fiend!" I shrieked, upstarting,—
"Get thee back into the tempest and the night's Plutonian shore!
Leave no black plume as a token of that lie thy should hath spoken!
Leave my loneliness unbroken!—quit the bust above my door!
Take thy beak from out my heart, and take thy form from off my door!"
        Quoth the raven, "Nevermore!"

And the raven, never flitting, still is sitting, still is sitting
On the pallid bust of Pallas just above my chamber door;
And his eyes have all the seeming of a demon that is dreaming,
And the lamplight o'er him streaming throws his shadow on the
    floor;
And my soul from out that shadow that lies floating on the floor
        Shall be lifted—*nevermore!*

Lo, Hear the Gentle Bloodhound!

I F BLOODHOUNDS COULD WRITE—all that these wonderful dogs can really do, and it's plenty, is trail lost children and old ladies, and track down lawbreakers and lunatics—they would surely be able to set down more demonstrable truths about themselves than Man has discovered in several centuries of speculation and guesswork, lighted only here and there with genuine research. Books about the St. Bernard, storied angel of the mountain snows, and the German shepherd and other breeds famous for their work as army scouts, city cops, and seeing-eye dogs, sprawl all over the library, but the literature of the English bloodhound, an even greater benefactor of mankind, is meager and sketchy. Only one standard book is available, *Bloodhounds and How to Train Them*, by Dr. Leon F. Whitney of New Haven, first published in 1947 and brought out in a revised edition a few months ago.

Man doesn't even know for sure how the bloodhound got his name. Dr. Whitney, veterinarian, geneticist, and researcher, and many other authorities, subscribe to the respectable theory that the "blood" is short for "blooded," meaning a patrician, an aristocrat, a thoroughbred. My own theory is that the "blood" got into the name because of the ancient English superstition that giants and other monsters, including the hound with the Gothic head and the miraculously acute nose, could smell the blood of their prey. The giant that roared, "I smell the blood of an Englishman!" had the obscene legendary power, in my opinion, to smell blood through clothing and flesh. Nobody knows to this day the source, nature, or chemistry of the aura that sets off each human being from all others in the sensitive nostrils of every type of scent-hound, but we will get around to that profound mystery further along on this trail. It seems to me, however, that legend and lore are more likely than early breeders and fanciers to have given the bloodhound his name. In any case, it has always had a fearsome sound to the ignorant ear, and one of the gentlest of all species, probably, indeed, the gentlest, has been more maligned through the centuries than any other great Englishman with the exception of King Richard the Third.

Dictionaries, encyclopedias, and other imposing reference volumes approach the bloodhound with an air of gingerly insecurity. *Webster's International*, touching lightly on the subject, observes, truly enough, that the bloodhound was originally used for hunting game, and adds "especially wounded game." This phrase may have grown out of the imperishable legend of blood scent, but it is also based on the fact that bloodhounds were ever slow and ponderous pursuers, more apt to catch up with a wounded stag or a stricken hart than one of unimpaired fleetness. The staid *Encyclopedia Britannica* gives our hero scant attention and alludes vaguely to an Italian type of the third century, a scent-hound, without doubt, but not a genuine bloodhound. There were scent-hounds, Dr. Whitney's researches prove, as far back as the age of Xenophon in Greece. Incidentally, the dogs that hunt by sight instead of smell, eminently the swift greyhound, originated, according to Webster, as long ago as 1300 B.C.

The sight-hounds have enjoyed, through the ages, a romantic tradition, for it is this type of canine hunter that has immemorially appeared in fairy tales, leading the mounted king and his three sons in swift pursuit of the fleet deer which turns out in the end to be an enchanted princess. But the scent-hounds of fiction have usually been terrifying creatures, and they have done their share in bringing libel to the fair name of the bloodhound. The terrible phosphorescent Hound of the Baskervilles, which terrorized the moors and bedeviled Sherlock Holmes and Dr. Watson, was a purebred Conan Doyle hound, but if you ask the average person to identify it, he will almost always say that it was a bloodhound, as savage as all the rest of the breed. Let us sniff a little further along the trail of reference volumes, before setting out on the ancient spoor of the bloodhound itself. The austere *Oxford English Dictionary* doesn't even attempt to account for the bloodhound's name, but with its famous bloodhound ability to track down sources, comes up with these variants of the name, used in England from 1350 through the eighteenth century: "blod-hounde, bloode hownde, blude hunde, blood hunde, bloud-hound, blod-honde." The name was spelled the way it is today by Oliver Goldsmith, Sir Walter Scott, John Keats ("The wakeful bloodhound rose, and shook his hide"), and Lord Byron, who once wrote "To have set the bloodhound mob on their patrician prey." Here the great hunter is no longer a patrician himself, but he hunts only patricians, as the Belvidere foxhounds, drawn years ago by D. T. Carlisle for *The Sportsman*, hunted only silver fox. The O. E. D., by the way, adds "stolen cattle" to the blood-hound's ancient quarry of wounded stags, wanted criminals, and wandering children. It could have brought the record up to date by putting lost dogs in the list, and at least one cat, which disappeared in an Eastern town not long ago and was found by a bloodhound that had sniffed its sandbox and followed the feline trail faithfully but with ponderous embarrassment, I feel sure.

The first scent-hound, or expert private nose, that stands out clearly in the tapestry of time is the St. Hubert of France, in the eighth century. Some of these castle-and-monastery hounds, after 1066, were imported into England, and from them sprang three English types, the talbot, the staghound, and the bloodhound. Of these, only the bloodhound remains extant. The infamous libel that clings to his name, the legend that he is a dog of awful ferocity began, in this country, before the Civil War, when foxhounds and mongrels were used to hunt down escaped slaves and were trained to fierceness. There may have been a few purebred English bloodhounds in Virginia and other southern states a hundred years ago, but the dogs that pursued Eliza across the ice in *Uncle Tom's Cabin* were crossbred, bar-sinister hounds. It was such beasts that tracked down members of James Andrew's Northern Raiders after they had stolen the famous Iron Horse locomotive at Big Shanty, Georgia, and finally took to the woods of the Southern Confederacy. These inferior pursuers could be bought for five dollars a pair, but the purebred bloodhound then cost fifty dollars a pair. The reputation of the mongrels for ferocity was calculated to deter slaves from making a break for freedom, for if they did and were caught by the dogs, they were sometimes mangled or killed. The trail of a fugitive slave was usually fresh, and any nose-hound could follow it easily. This is also true of the trails of prisoners who escape from prison farms and penitentiaries today, and therefore the so-called penitentiary hounds do not need the educated nostrils of a thoroughbred. They are also trained to fierceness, since they must often deal with dangerous criminals.

However the "blood" may have got into our hero's name, it has helped to stain him almost indelibly as a cruel and feral monster. The miraculous finder of lost boys and girls, the brilliant finger-man of thousands of sheriffs' posses, policemen, and private trailers, could be safely trusted not to harm a babe in arms. Dr. Whitney's bloodhounds once found a three-year-old Connecticut girl who had wandered away from her grandmother in a deep bramble of blackberry bushes. The dogs insisted on searching an almost impenetrable swampy region, but were deterred for hours by *Homo sapiens*, in uniform and out, who was positive the child could not have gone that far. When the human beings finally gave the dogs their own way, they dashed into the thicket. Half an hour later the hunting men came upon the little girl, sitting in a pool of water—she had taken off her playsuit to go for a swim. She was naked as a jay bird, but happy as a lark because of the two lovely wrinkled canine playmates she had just "found." Without the help of the hounds, she could never have been traced.

The *Oxford Dictionary*, with its characteristic erudition, reports that the bloodhound's Latin name is *canis sanguinarius*, a name the Romans never used. Now *sanguinarius* does not mean blooded, in the sense of purebred; it means of or pertaining to blood, and, figuratively, bloody, bloodthirsty, sanguinary. The gentle, good-tempered, well-balanced bloodhound is actually about as fierce as Little Eva, and you simply cannot discover one provable instance of a bloodhound's attacking a child or an adult, including a cornered criminal. Dr. Whitney says the hounds don't even seem to know that teeth were made for biting. It is true that one bloodhound I heard about became understandably vexed when his master pulled him off a hot trail, and showed his indignation by a thunderous growl. It is unwise to frustrate a bloodhound who has not come to the end of a trail he is following, and how could this one have known that the bandit he was after had been apprehended, according to a telephone call, fifteen miles ahead?

It has been nearly twenty years since I came upon a flagrant piece of calumny about my friend the bloodhound, in a four-volume set of books called *The Outline of Science, a Plain Story Simply Told,* but my indignation is still as strong as it was then. The anonymous "expert" assigned to write about canines in these books had this to say: "There are few dogs which do not inspire affection; many crave it. But there are some which seem to repel us, like the bloodhound. True, Man has made him what he is. Terrible to look at and terrible to encounter, Man has raised him up to hunt down his fellowman." Accompanying the article was a picture of a dignified and melancholy English bloodhound, about as terrible to look at as Abraham Lincoln, about as terrible to encounter as Jimmy Durante. It pleases me no end that this passage, in its careless use of English, accidentally indicts the human being: "Terrible to look at and terrible to encounter, Man. . . ." Even my beloved, though occasionally cockeyed, Lydekker's *New Natural History,* whose grizzy-bear expert pooh-poohs the idea that grizzly bears are dangerous (it seems they got the reputation of aggressiveness by rolling downhill toward the hunter after they were shot dead), knows better than to accuse the bloodhound of viciousness, or, at any rate, has the good sense to avoid the subject of his nature. Lydekker's bloodhound man contents himself with a detailed and fascinating physical description of the breed, which goes like this. "The most striking and characteristic feature of the bloodhound is its magnificent head, which is considerably larger and heavier in the male than in the female. While generally extremely massive, the head is remarkable for its narrowness between the ears, where it rises into a domelike prominence, terminating in a marked protuberance in the occipital region. The skin of the forehead, like that round the eyes, is thrown into a series of transverse puckers." The Lydekker dog man alludes, in conclusion, to what he calls "a foreign strain of the bloodhound, which is lower on its legs than the English breed."

This foreigner could not possibly be the hound I have been putting into drawings for twenty-five years, because I was only six when the first American edition of Lydekker's *History* was brought out. My dog *is* lower on its legs than a standard bloodhound, although I would scarcely put it that way myself. He got his short legs by accident. I drew him for the first time on the cramped pages of a small memo pad in order to plague a busy realtor friend of mine given to writing down names and numbers while you were trying to talk to him in his office. The hound I draw has a fairly accurate pendulous ear, but his dot of an eye is vastly oversimplified, he doesn't have enough transverse puckers, and he is all wrong in the occipital region. He may not be as keen as a genuine bloodhound, but his heart is just as gentle; he does not want to hurt anybody or anything; and he loves serenity and heavy dinners, and wishes they would go on forever, like the brook.

The late Hendrik Van Loon is the only man I have known well who owned a bloodhound, but he took his back to the kennel where he had bought it, after trying in vain to teach it something besides the fine art of pursuit. Whenever Mr. Van Loon called the dog, he once told me sorrowfully, it took its own good time finding him, although he might be no more than fifty feet away. This bloodhound never went directly to his master, but conscientiously followed his rambling trail. "He was not interested in me or where I was," said Mr. Van Loon. "All he cared about was how I had got there." Mr. Van Loon had made the mistake of assuming that a true bloodhound would fit as cozily into a real living room as my hound does in the drawings. It is a mistake to be sedulously avoided. "I would rather housebreak a moose," the great man told me with a sigh.

The English bloodhound has never been one of the most popular housedogs in the world, but this is not owing solely to the dark slander that has blackened his reputation. He is a large, enormously evident creature, likely to make a housewife fear for her antiques and draperies, and he is not given to frolic and parlor games. He is used to the outdoors. If you want a dog to chase a stick or a ball, or jump through a hoop, don't look at him. "Bloodhounds ain't any good unless you're lost," one little boy told me scornfully. It must be admitted that the cumbersome, jowly tracer of lost persons is somewhat blobbered and slubby (you have to make up words for unique creatures like the bloodhound and the bandersnatch). Compared to breeds whose members are numbered in multiple thousands, the bloodhound is a rare variety, and there may not be more than 1,500 or 2,000 of them in America. An accurate census is discouraged by some bloodhound kennels, many of which are not listed in the *American Kennel Gazette* for their own protection. Some years ago a Connecticut pack of twenty was poisoned, presumably by a friend or relative of some lawbreaker that one or two of the hounds had tracked down. The hounds are bred for two main purposes: to be exhibited at dog shows around the country, and to be trained for police work or private investigation. In 1954, at the annual Eastern Dog Club Show in Boston, a five-year-old bloodhound named Fancy Bombardier was selected as the best dog of all the breeds assembled there, for the first time in the forty-one-year history of the show. This was a rare distinction for our friend, for it was one of the infrequent times a bloodhound in this country ever went Best of Show. Not many judges are as familiar with the show points of a bloodhound as they are with the simpler ones of other breeds. The wondrous Englishman, with his voluminous excess wrinkled flesh, his cathedral head and hooded, pink-hawed eyes, deep-set in their sockets, might seem to some judges too grotesque for prizes, but these are his marks of merit and aristocracy.

Bloodhound-owners themselves disagree about bloodhound types and their comparative appeal, the orthodox school vehemently contending that the purebred hound is the favorite of dog-show galleries, the other school contending that the old patricians repel visitors and are frequently regarded as "hideous." There may yet be a well-defined feud between the two schools. Dr. Whitney, geneticist, eugenicist, and mammalogist, among other things, is one of those who approve of the so-called American-type bloodhound, whose anatomy is less exaggerated. Its "streamlined" conformation is said to be a virtue in trailing, if not an advantage in the show ring. Some authorities believe that this American hound, if judiciously crossbred with the English type, would add a morganatic strain of sturdiness to the Grand Duke's descendants. The English dog, after centuries of pure breeding, does not have a powerful constitution and is subject to certain virus infections and a destructive stomach ailment called "bloat." (Six fine American-owned bloodhounds died of it last year.)

Many state police barracks, but far from enough, have at least one pair of trained bloodhounds. Perhaps the foremost police trainer and trailer in the East is Sergeant W. W. Horton of the state barracks at Hawthorne, New York. He began years ago as a corporal, and for nearly two decades he and his dogs have built up a great record tracking down the crooked and the vanished. They have worked in half a dozen different states, and three years ago Sergeant Horton and his partner were asked by the government of Bermuda to bring their dogs down there to hunt a criminal, notorious for his escapes from prison and his skill in hiding out. They were the first bloodhounds that most Bermudians had seen, and they were not warmly welcomed by the population because of the ancient superstitions about them. The dogs found the coral terrain of Bermuda a good scent-holder, but they were disturbed by crowds of people that followed them, like a gallery at a golf tournament. They traced their man, finally, down to the water's edge, where he had apparently escaped from the island by ship. Sergeant Horton and his partner wore holstered .38 police pistols which astonished the Bermudians, who may keep guns in their homes, but wouldn't dream of displaying one in public. "They thought we were making a movie," Sergeant Horton told me the other day. "Everybody kept looking for the cameras." (I tracked the Sergeant down easily. He was handling the switchboard when I phoned.) Rusty, one of the two Hawthorne hounds that flew to Bermuda, died last winter at the unusual age of fifteen years.

The success of the dogs as trailers depends a great deal on what might be called the dogmanship of their trainers and handlers. Dr. Whitney, who has worked his own hounds with, and sometimes parallel to, the police of Connecticut, New York, and Rhode Island, has often found his man on cases in which official police dogs had failed. Expertness with a canine trailer is a knack, like a green thumb in the garden or a light hand in the kitchen, and some cops never get the hang of it. The training of a bloodhound may begin when the dog is a puppy, capable of toddling a trail only a few yards long, but a two-year-old beginner can sometimes be taught most of the tricks in six weeks; with others it may take six months. They may begin by watching a "runner" disappear from an automobile in which he has left his coat behind. The dog sniffs it carefully and sets out on the trail when the runner is lost to view. Youngsters are often used as runners, and they leave a blazed trail so that the handler can tell if the dogs get off the track. The handicap of time is slowly increased, and so is the number of runners. Eventually, five or more of them set out in single file and it is up to the bloodhound to follow the track of only one when the group scatters, the runner whose coat or cap or shoe the dog has examined with the sharpest nose in the world. He must learn to go up to a youngster whose shoe he has sniffed, paying no attention to another youngster, nearer at hand, who may be holding a piece of liver and smelling to high heaven of reward.

Bloodhounds have done more for humanity than all other canines and most men. Examples of their unique achievements would easily fill two sizable volumes, and I can only select a few at random. Let us begin with the late Madge, a bitch owned many years ago by Dr. C. Fosgate of Oxford, New York. Madge was once called upon to trace a lost boy in a town upstate. The trail was twenty-four hours old. Madge climbed fences, wandered through yards, went down alleys, and presently asked to be let into a grocery. Inside, she trotted to a crate of oranges, then crossed over and placed both front paws on the counter. The grocer then remembered that a little boy had come in the morning before, taken an orange from the crate, and paid for it at the counter. The end of the trail was tragic: Madge came to a pier end at a river and plunged unhesitatingly into the water. The boy had been drowned there.

For more than a quarter of a century, up to October 1954, to be exact, the record for following the coldest trail, 105 hours old, was held by a male named Nick Carter, generally considered to have been the greatest bloodhound that ever lived. He was part of the most fabulous pack of bloodhounds in our history, one belonging to the late Captain Volney G. Mullikin of Kentucky. An entire volume could be devoted to the Mullikin hounds alone, and to their colorful master. From about 1897 until 1932, the Mullikin hounds brought about the capture of 2,500 criminals and wrongdoers in Kentucky, Tennessee, West Virginia, and other states. A hundred of them were wanted for murder, others for rape, or burglary, or moonshining, or sabotage (Captain Mullikin got $5,000 from a West Virginia coal company for tracking down a gang of saboteurs), and almost every other crime in the calendar, including arson. Nick Carter's old cold trail of four days and nine hours brought to justice a man who had burned down a hen house, but he closed a total of six hundred cases, most of them major, during his great career, and no other dog has ever come close to that accomplishment. The Nick Carter case that I have encountered most often in my researches was one in which he brought to justice a group of mischievous youngsters who, for many weeks, had been in the habit of throwing rocks through the windows of houses at night and easily avoiding capture by the police. Nick was finally allowed to sniff one of the rocks which had been pulled out from under a bed with a cane and placed on a newspaper. Nick got the first of the young miscreants in a matter of hours, and the other boys were soon rounded up.

Captain Mullikin, whose photograph shows a lean, rangy, keen-eyed man, was brave to the point of foolhardiness, and more than once stood off lynching mobs, protecting a prisoner whose guilt had not been proved. He and his dogs were in the bloody midst of the Howard-Baker and Hatfield-McCoy mountain feuds, and ran to earth a number of assassins on both sides of each of these family wars. The captain's body showed scores of buckshot scars, most of them on his legs. The fame of the Kentucky pack and its valiant leader spread as far as Cuba, and the government of that island hired the Kentuckians, on a six-months' contract, to capture a notorious bandit. The hounds caught up with the man in a matter of days, but the Cuban government insisted on paying the full six-months' fee agreed upon.

When Captain Mullikin died, he left much of his blood-houndiana, including a mountain of newspaper clippings reciting the glorious feats of the captain and his dogs, to Dr. Whitney, to whose book I am indebted for these all too brief Mullikin facts. The doctor was also given the harness that had been worn by Nick Carter on his hundreds of cases. When a hound starts out on a trail, his leash is unfastened from his collar and snapped onto his harness, and this forms the go-ahead signal, along with some such invariable command as "Find him" or "Go get 'em." Incidentally, there are two kinds of working bloodhounds, known as open trailers—the ones that bay as they go—and mute trailers—the dogs that give no sign of their approach—and you can get into a rousing argument about comparative values in this field, too. Hounds of any kind hunting by themselves, alone or in pairs or packs, always bay on the trail of an animal quarry, but the leashed bloodhound can be taught either sound or silence in trailing a human being. No bloodhound ever gives tongue when he gets off the scent, which, it should be pointed out, is by no means the mere width of a footprint, but can sometimes be picked up by the dogs over an area of a hundred feet or more.

I called one day on the eight bloodhounds owned by Thomas Sheahan, a factory worker and past president of the American Bloodhound Club, which has only seventy members and is now headed by Mrs. Clendenin J. Ryan. One of hers, Champion Rye of Panther Ledge, beat out Mr. Sheahan's Fancy Bombardier for best of breed at a show last April. Fancy and Rye had met a number of times, however, and the former holds the edge in victories. The Sheahan hounds are neighbors of mine, kenneled at Torrington, twenty miles away. The chief of the pack is, of course, Fancy Bombardier, a couchant hound in the best tradition of austere and pensive Rodinesque posture. A grown poodle poses with the professional grace of an actress, but a bloodhound resembles a Supreme Court Justice gravely submitting to the indignity of being photographed. Bloodhounds may look exactly alike to the layman, but they are not turned out of a rigid mold, like cast-iron lawn dogs. Bombardier's son, Essex Tommy, whose late grandfather had a fine trailing record with the Bethany State Police Barracks in Connecticut, is a wag, a gayheart, with the bloodhound habit of rearing up and planting his big friendly paws on your chest. This affable bloodhound mannerism has been known to frighten a cornered culprit, who does not realize his big pursuer merely wants to shake hands, like the American colonel that captured Hermann Goering at the end of the war.

The Sheahan hounds are bred for show, not trailing, although a few have joined the Connecticut State Police. One of the hounds kept digging solemnly deep into the ground while I was there, hunting for the roots of a tree, which all dogs love to chew. A nine-month-old female got into a loud altercation with a fourteen-year-old German shepherd—something about a missing bone—but there was no biting, only argument and accusation. As puppies, bloodhounds are almost as playful as other dogs, but they soon become sedentary and are interested in no game except professional hide-and-seek. They are brought up outdoors, to thicken their coats and toughen them, but they have to be introduced to rough weather gradually. Once acclimatized, a sound dog may be able to sleep in the snow without chill or frostbite. They are neither climbers nor jumpers, and often have to be lifted over fences and other obstacles. Worn out after a long trail, they may have to be carried and fall asleep easily in their trainers' arms. Mr. Sheahan pulled down the lower eyelid of one patient bloodhound, to show its deep-set reddish eye, which seems to be slowly on its way to becoming vestigial. The stronger the nose, the weaker the eye, generally speaking, and blood-hounds sometimes bump into things on a trail. "You shouldn't be able to see a bloodhound's eye at a distance of thirty feet," Mr. Sheahan said. This is a show point in a true bloodhound's favor. Bloodhounds have a short vocabulary, and few changes of inflec-tion or intonation. Fancy Bombardier kept saying "Who?" deep-ening the volume as his questioning went on. "*Who?*" he demanded. "Ralph!" I barked. "*Who?*" he roared. "Ralph Ralph Rolf," I said, and so the stolid cross-examination continued.

The bloodhound is not a commercial dog, and few kennel owners break even financially. A good male puppy usually brings about a hundred dollars, rarely more than three hundred, and eight hundred to a thousand dollars is a high price nowadays for a trained adult of either sex. The first bloodhounds brought into this country from England in this century, around 1905, included some that had cost from $2,000 to $3,000. The prices got lower as the popularity of the breed slowly began to decline. It has come up sharply in recent years, but even so, only 195 new blood-hounds were registered with the American Kennel Club last year. Thomas Sheahan and another eminent bloodhound man, Clar-ence Fischer of Kingston, New York, recently recommended a $550 perfect male specimen to George Brooks of LaCrosse, Wisconsin, who bought the dog on their say-so without having seen it. Mr. Fischer, whom some of his colleagues call the most dedicated bloodhound man in America, if not the world, owns the finest and most extensive collection of bloodhoundiana in the country, and has known personally most of the leading American owners and trainers. George Brooks, who works in a drugstore when he is not on the trail, is considered one of the outstanding tracers. His dogs often work at night, since they are less distracted by sights and sounds, and young dogs just learning the trade do much better in the dark. The Brooks hounds specialize in city trailing, and their services are often required by police departments in the Middle West, but they can take on a country job and do just as well. Last winter they followed the tragic trail of two little boys to a hole in the ice of a river where they had drowned.

Most of the trails of lost children and adults fortunately end in the discovery of the persons alive and well. Some police authorities approve of perpetuating the libel that a bloodhound is a savage beast, accustomed to tearing his quarry to bits when he comes upon it. The purpose of this wrong-minded philosophy is to deter evil-doers, and make them think twice before committing a crime and seeking to escape. It is a badly thought-out reversion to the theory and practice of southern slaveowners a hundred years ago and, the point of morality aside, it is calculated to cause the parents of wandering children to fear the use of bloodhounds.

There is a widespread belief, among the uninitiated, that the bloodhound's usefulness in tracking down criminals came to an end with the era of the automobile and the advent of the getaway car. This is only partly true. It is common knowledge that our olfactory genius is interested in automobiles only for what they may contain in the way of human odors, and could not possibly tell a Buick from a Packard, or one tire from another. Everybody also knows that no hound, even if it were able to follow a tire trail, could trace an automobile over hundreds or thousands of miles. But these self-evident facts by no means completely hamstring or footcuff the relentless pursuers. Many fleeing criminals abandon their cars sooner or later, usually alongside a wooded area, thus becoming a setup for bloodhounds. The dogs will get into an abandoned car, inhale a long snoutful of evidence, and set out gleefully and confidently on the track into the woods. They can tell more about the driver or other occupants of an empty motorcar than the police experts in any laboratory. And, remarkable to say, bloodhounds have been known to follow the hot, short trail of a car by picking up, some yards off the road, the scent of the fugitive, if they have previously been able to sniff some personal belonging of his. One hound trotted in a ditch, parallel to the highway, for four miles, apparently detecting with ease the scent of his quarry, car or no car. This particular fugitive had made the mistake of turning into a driveway, four miles from his point of departure, and there was the car, and there was the man, and there, finally, was the hound, ready to shake hands and be congratulated.

This is probably the point at which I should dwell, briefly and in all bewilderment, upon just what it is that human scent consists of. All anybody seems to know is that the distinctive human smell the bloodhound selects from all others must have the infinite variability of fingerprints. Only the bloodhound comprehends this scent, which is so sharp to him and so mysterious to us, and all he has ever said about it is "Who?" Some bloodhound men think of the scent as a kind of effluvium, an invisible exudation that clings low to the earth, about the footprints of men. Whatever it may be, a few facts are definitely known about certain of its manifestations. Dampness, especially that of light rain or dew, often serves to bring out the scent, and it is further preserved by "cover," which, in the argot of the trailer, means underbrush, thicket, low-spreading plants and bushes, and the like. Bloodhounds are frequently handicapped by what is technically known as the "fouling" of a trail by sightseers and other careless humans. Wind also adds to the troubles of a hound, along with thoughtless trampling by men, in the case of a hunt over snow. One of the hounds belonging to Mr. and Mrs. Robert Noerr of Stamford, Connecticut, is now working out of Anchorage, Alaska, helping to find persons lost in the snows.

The 105-hour record for cold trailing, so long held by the celebrated Nick Carter, was shattered in October 1954 by the well-nigh incredible achievement of three bloodhounds belonging to Norman W. Wilson of Los Gatos, California, a former navy pilot who dedicated himself to the training of bloodhounds after a friend of his had become lost in the Everglades and was found by some Florida hounds. On October 9, 1954, a man and his wife and their thirteen-year-old son went deer hunting in a heavily wooded region of Oregon, thick with second-growth fir and a dense undergrowth of ferns and brush. Just a week later their car was found parked near the woods. The sheriff of the county, aided by two hundred men, an airplane and a helicopter, searched the almost impenetrable area without avail for six days. Wilson and his dogs arrived by plane, and the dogs picked up the ancient scent near the car, using as a scent guide a pair of the wife's stockings. Their leashes were fastened to their harness and the command "Find them!" was given at 9:45 on the night of October 22, 322 hours after the family was thought to have left their car. The dogs "cast" in wide circles, trying to pick up the trail, until three o'clock the next morning, and resumed the search shortly after six o'clock. There had been rains on the night of October 10 and later, and the underbrush and ferns were wet. Fifteen hours after they had taken up the search, or 337 hours after the supposed entrance of the family into the woods, one of the hounds led its trainer to the body of the youngster. The parents were subsequently found, also dead. Mr. Wilson and the sheriff and other officials later submitted the story of the remarkable search, in affidavit form, to the Bloodhound Club, and it seems likely that the amazing new record will be officially accepted. The hounds had led the human searchers in a different direction from that which the sheriff and his two hundred men had taken, in their own dogless and fruitless search. Mr. Wilson, it should be said, receives no reward for his services and those of his hounds, beyond the expenses involved in a hunt. He had offered to help after reading about the missing persons in the newspapers. Nobody had thought to send for bloodhounds.

Curiously enough, no bloodhound man seems ever to have experimented to find out how many hours, or days, or perhaps even months or years, the scent of a man or a woman or a child might still cling to something that had once been worn. It is an obvious and interesting area of research, and I am sure the dogs would love it.

One of my favorite bloodhounds is Symbol of Kenwood, a two-year-old from one of the excellent kennels on the West Coast, and a member of the New Mexico Mounted Patrol. Last December Symbol traced two men, wanted for the murder of an Albuquerque policeman, down to the edge of the Rio Grande, promptly hit the water and swam across the river and pointed out his men. They had thought the broad expanse of water would frustrate any pursuing bloodhound. Symbol's feat made up for his impish delinquency of a few days earlier, when he had dug his way out of his kennel and wandered off. He was gone for forty-eight hours, and members of the Mounted Patrol looked for him in vain. He came home, finally, in excellent spirits, having presumably backtracked his own trail. He must have had a twinkle in his grave deep-set eyes as he rejoined the tired and baffled patrol, and I hoped he wasn't punished too much. Everybody probably had his own theory as to where Symbol had gone, and everybody was wrong, as Man so often is in dealing with the bloodhound breed. These patient dogs have used, many a time and oft, their one monosyllabic interrogation in dialogue with men, who think their own wisdom is so superior. I wish I could be present some day to hear one of these man-and-dog conversations. Let us say that a parent, or a police officer, or a posse man is speaking first, like this:

"No child could possibly have got through that hedge, according to Sheriff Spencer and Police Chief MacGowan."

"Who?"

And here, gentle reader, let us leave our amazing hero, with the last, and only truly authoritative word.

Mr. Monroe Holds
the Fort

THE COUNTRY HOUSE, on this particular wintry afternoon, was most enjoyable. Night was trudging up the hill and the air was sharp. Mr. Monroe had already called attention several times to the stark beauty of the black tree branches limned, as he put it, against the sky. The wood fire had settled down to sleepy glowing in the grate.

"It *is* a little lonely, though," said Mrs. Monroe. (The nearest house was far away.)

"I love it," said her husband, darkly. At moments and in places like this, he enjoyed giving the impression of a strong, silent man wrapped in meditation. He stared, brooding, into the fire. Mrs. Monroe, looking quite tiny and helpless, sat on the floor at his feet and leaned against him. He gave her shoulder two slow, reflective pats.

"I really don't mind staying here when Germaine is here—just we two," said Mrs. Monroe, "but I think I would be terrified if I were alone." Germaine, the maid, a buxom, fearless woman, was in town on shopping leave. The Monroes had thought it would be fun to spend the weekend alone and get their own meals, the way they used to.

"There's nothing in the world to be afraid of," said Mr. Monroe.

"Oh, it gets so terribly black outside, and you hear all kinds of funny noises at night that you don't hear during the day." Mr. Monroe explained to her why that was—expansion (said he) of woodwork in the cold night air, and so on. From there he somehow went into a discussion of firearms, which would have betrayed to practically anyone that his knowledge of guns was limited to a few impressive names like Colt and Luger. They were one of those things he was always going to read up on but never did. He mentioned quietly, however, that he was an excellent shot.

"Mr. Farrington left his pistol here, you know," said Mrs. Monroe, "but I've never touched it—ugh!"

"He did?" cried her husband. "Where is it? I'd like to take a look at it." Mr. Farrington was the man from whom they had taken, on long lease, the Connecticut place.

"It's upstairs in the chest of drawers in the back room," said Mrs. Monroe. Her husband, despite her protests, went up and got it and brought it down. "Please put it away!" said his wife. "Is it loaded? Oh, don't do that! Please!" Mr. Monroe, looking grim and competent, was aiming the thing, turning it over, scowling at it.

"It's loaded all right," he said, "all five barrels."

"Chambers," said his wife.

"Yes," he said. "Let me show you how to use it—after all, you can never tell when you're going to need a gun."

"Oh, I'd never use it—even if one of those convicts that escaped yesterday came right up the stairs and I could shoot him, I'd just stand there. I'd be *paralyzed!*"

"Nonsense!" said Mr. Monroe. "You don't have to shoot a man. Get the drop on him, stand him up with his face against a wall, and phone the police. Look here—" he covered an imaginary figure, backed him against the wall, and sat down at the phone table. "Always keep your eye on him; don't look into the transmitter." Mr. Monroe glared at his man, lifted up the receiver, holding the hook down with his finger, and spoke quietly to the phone. In the midst of this the phone rang. Mr. Monroe started sharply.

"It's for you, dear," he said presently. His wife took the receiver.

How curiously things happen! That is what Mr. Monroe thought, an hour later, as he drove back from the station after taking his wife there to catch the seven-ten. Imagine her mother getting one of those fool spells at this time! Imagine expecting a grown daughter to come running every time you felt a little dizzy! Imagine—well, the ways of women were beyond him. He turned into the drive of the country house. Judas, but it was dark! Dark and silent. Mr. Monroe didn't put the machine in the garage. He got out and stood still, listening. Off toward the woods somewhere he heard a thumping noise. Partridge drumming, thought Mr. Monroe. But partridge didn't thump, they whirred—didn't they? Oh, well, they probably thumped at this time of year.

It was good to get inside the house. He built up the fire, and turned on the overhead lights—his wife never allowed them turned on. Then he went into a couple of other rooms and turned on more lights. He wished he had gone in town with her. Of course she'd be back in the morning on the ten-ten and they'd have the rest of that day—Sunday—together. Still . . . he went to the drawer where he had put the revolver and got it out. He fell to wondering whether the thing would work. Long-unused guns often jammed, or exploded. He went out into the kitchen, carrying the pistol. His wife had told him to be sure and get himself a snack. He opened the refrigerator door, looked in, decided he wasn't hungry, and closed it again. He went back to the living room and began to pace up and down. He decided to put the pistol on the mantel, butt toward him. Then he practiced making quick grabs for it. Presently he sat down in a chair, picked up a *Nation* and began to read, at random: "Two men are intimately connected with the killing of striking workers at Marion, North Carolina. . . ." Where had those convicts his wife mentioned escaped from? Dannemora? Matteawan? How far were those places from this house? Maybe having all the lights on was a bad idea. He got up and turned the upper lights off; and then turned them on again . . . There was a step outside. Crunch! crunch! . . . Mr. Monroe hurried to the mantel, knocked the gun on to the floor, fumbled for it, and stuck it in a hip pocket just as a knock sounded at the door.

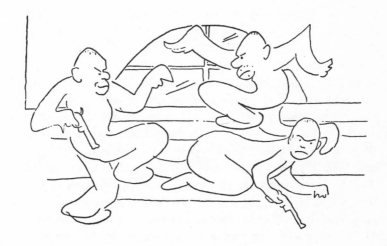

Burglars flitting about in the attic of a house in which the master is home alone.

"Wha—" began Mr. Monroe, and was surprised to find he couldn't say anything else. The knocking continued. He stepped to the door, stood far to one side, and said, "Yeh?" A cheery voice responded. Reassured, Mr. Monroe opened the door. A motorist wanted to know how to get to the Wilton road. Mr. Monroe told him, speaking quiet loudly. Afterward, lifted up by this human contact, he went back to his reading in the *Nation*: Around one-thirty one of the foremen approached young Luther Bryson, 22, one of the victims, and harangued him: "If you strike this time, you—, we will shoot it out with you . . ." Mr. Monroe put the magazine down. He got up and went to the Victrola, selected a jazz record, and began to play it. It occurred to him that if there were steps outside, he couldn't hear them. He shut the machine off. The abrupt silence made him still, listening. He heard all kinds of noises. One of them came from upstairs—a quick, sliding noise, like a convict slipping into a clothes closet . . . the fellow had a beard and a blue-steel gun . . . a man in the dark had the advantage. Mr. Monroe's mouth began to feel stuffy. "Damn it! This can't go on!" he said aloud, and felt bucked up. Then someone put his heel down sharply on the floor just above. Mr. Monroe tentatively picked up a flashlight, and pulled the pistol from his pocket. The phone rang sharply. "Good God!" said Mr. Monroe, backing against a wall. He slid on to the chair in front of the phone, with the gun in his right hand, and took up the receiver with his left. When he spoke into the transmitter his eyes kept roving around the room. "H'lo," he said. It was Mrs. Monroe. Her mother was all right. Was he all right? He was fine. What was he doing? Oh, reading. (He kept the gun trained on the foot of the steps leading upstairs.) Well, what would he think if she came back out on that midnight train? Her mother was all right. Would he be too sleepy to wait up and meet her? Hell, no! That was fine! Do that! . . .

Mr. Monroe hung up the receiver with a profound sigh of relief. He looked at his watch. Hm, wouldn't have to leave for the station for nearly two hours. Whistling, he went out to the refrigerator (still carrying the gun) and fetched out the butter and some cold meat. He made a couple of sandwiches (laying the gun on the kitchen table) and took them into the living room (putting the gun in his pocket). He turned off the overhead lights, sat down, picked up a *Harper's* and began to read. Abruptly, that flitting, clothes-closety sound came from upstairs again. Mr. Monroe finished his sandwiches hurriedly, with the gun on his lap, got up, went from room to room turning off the extra lights, put on his hat and overcoat, locked several doors, went out and got into his car. After all, he could read just as well at the station, and he would be sure of being there on time—might fall asleep otherwise. He started the engine, and whirled out of the drive. He felt for the pistol, which was in his overcoat pocket. He would slip it into the chest of drawers upstairs later on. Mr. Monroe came to a crossroads and a light. He began to whistle.

Little Joe

(Suggested by the latest gunman fiction, and several other things)

I

ANGELINO STOOD at the window, looking down into Broadway.
He fiddled with his watchfob nervously. This was the first
job he had ever pulled in New York, and it wasn't pulled yet. He
was fat, with a bald head, and he breathed with difficulty. He had
never been out of Chicago before in his life. From time to time he
studied his face in an ivory-backed hand-mirror.

"Well, let's get goin'," said the Turk. He was big, with a brown
face, and his index fingers twitched.

"All set," said Joe. Joe was little and pale, with beautiful black
hair.

"You guys got the layout?" asked Angelino.

"Everything's jake," said Joe.

"It's sure easy enough," said Angelino. "You walk straight into
the lobby, buy your tickets, and he's the first doorman you come
to, inside. Not the guy on the sidewalk, the guy at the inner
door—goes into the theater. The lobby'll be crowded with a lot of
yaps and nobody will pay no attention. Joe gives him the gun,
against the ribs—keep it inside your pocket, Joe—and the Turk
takes off his clothes—"

"To hell with that," said the Turk.

"You take off the *doorman's* clothes," said Joe.

"I get you," said the Turk, mollified.

"Don't bother about rippin' off the braid and the jewels—take

130

his whole damn suit," said Angelino. "We'll get the braid and the other stuff off later, back here, and split it three ways. That's all—only no gunplay. I don't want no gunplay. Get that."

"Come on, come on," said Joe, irritably. He started for the door. Angelino stopped to pick up his hand-mirror from the table and started to put it in his pocket.

"Lay off that damn lookin' glass," said Joe. Angelino put the mirror down.

"On our way, boys," he said briskly.

II

The lobby of the Movie Cathedral was crowded, mostly with young women and their escorts, chewing gum, laughing gaily. It was a quarter of nine. The crowd surged against the doorman every time anyone came out of the darkened theater.

"Standing room only, no seats," said the doorman.

"To hell with that," said the Turk. "I got a ticket, ain't I?"

"We got tickets," said Joe, pushing closer.

"There are no seats, just now," said the doorman. He wore a long silver-colored coat and trousers, with a great deal of solid-gold braid. A fourragère of gold, over one shoulder, was secured by a large emerald brooch in a handsome platinum setting. The coat buttons were also emeralds, somewhat smaller, but of equal purity, and the whole was charmingly set off by cuff stripes and trouser stripes of gold leaf, and surmounted, in exquisite taste, by a heavily braided cap, encrusted with rubies. A sunburst of diamonds formed the buckle of his wide crimson sash. The Turk eyed the ensemble greedily and his fingers twitched.

"Who dressed *you* up?" snarled the Turk, who had never seen anything like this in Chicago.

"Shut up, Turk," said Angelino. He pulled a hand-mirror from his pocket.

"I thought I told you to leave that thing at the hideout," said Joe.

"This is another one," said Angelino. He liked to look at himself.

"Nice bunch of softies I got in with," muttered Joe. He shoved up against the doorman and jabbed his gun against the doorman's hip.

"All quiet," said Joe. "You got a rod up against you, brother."

"Standing room only, no seats," said the doorman, who did not understand what Joe was talking about.

"I'm roddin' you, you fool," said Joe, fiercely. The Turk pushed up, ready to take the doorman's uniform off.

"If you will bear with the Civic Service a moment later, Civic Service will procure you seats," said the doorman.

"What's he say?" demanded the Turk. The Turk did not understand English very well. He could speak it, but he couldn't understand it very well.

"He says wait," said Angelino.

"To hell with that," said the Turk. He grabbed the doorman's coat and trousers and began pulling on them. The coat, being of solid-silver mesh, wouldn't rip easily. The three men had not foreseen this.

"Get a load o' that—the coat's made o' iron!" said the Turk.

"Silver!" breathed Joe.

"Get the braid! Jerk out the rocks! Knock off his hat!" shouted Angelino.

"Here! Here!" said the doorman. "Civic Service will not—"

"Keep your shirt on," said the Turk, menacingly. He grabbed a handful of the gold braid that encircled the doorman's shoulders and tore it off. Joe helped him with his free hand and began wrenching off jewels.

"Here! Here!" said the doorman. He reached for his hip, to keep his trousers up, but the Turk misunderstood the move. He fired from the hip. The doorman ran a few steps, looked as if he were about to sing something, and fell down.

"Let's get out of here!" said Joe. The three ran out of the lobby, knocking people down.

III

Angelino stood staring down at his baggage, waiting for the gates at Grand Central to open. He was nervous. Joe sat on his suitcases, smoking a cigarette, with his eyes closed. The Turk was staring at the women going by.

"Nice dames here," said the Turk.

"They'll get us for this," said Angelino.

"You're gettin' soft," said Joe. A policeman sauntered up.

"Take it easy," whispered Joe. The policeman went by.

"They'll get us sure for this," said Angelino. The gates opened. Angelino hurried forward. Just then a boy ran by shouting an extra. Joe whistled to him, and bought one. The three pushed through the gates.

IV

Joe gave up reading the paper, lay back against his seat, and closed his eyes.

"Have they got it?" said Angelino.

"Sure they got it," said Joe. Angelino put up his mirror, reached over, and took the paper from Joe. There were big headlines.

"What's it say?" asked the Turk. Angelino began to read.

"'Police believe that in the shooting of John Wells, movie-theater doorman, last night, they are confronted by an underworld plot whose roots may run deep into the byways and crannies of race-track gambling, night-club ownership, federal-prohibition-protection graft, and beer-war enmity. They are looking for a chorus girl known as Sad Emma, the manager of a notorious cabaret in the West Fifties, and several noted Broadway racketeers, who are said to hold the key to the mystery. The search may lead as far south as Miami and as far north as Bar Harbor and—'"

"To hell with that," said the Turk. The train pulled out of the tunnel, into the light. The three looked out at the city.

"Nice town to visit," said Joe.

"Yeah," said the Turk.

"A guy wouldn't want to live here, though," said Angelino.

The White Rabbit Caper

(As the Boys Who Turn Out the Mystery Programs on the Air Might Write a Story for Children)

F RED FOX was pouring himself a slug of rye when the door of his office opened and in hopped old Mrs. Rabbit. She was a white rabbit with pink eyes, and she wore a shawl on her head, and gold-rimmed spectacles.

"I want you to find Daphne," she said tearfully, and she handed Fred Fox a snapshot of a white rabbit with pink eyes that looked to him like a picture of every other white rabbit with pink eyes.

"When did she hop the hutch?" asked Fred Fox.

"Yesterday," said old Mrs. Rabbit. "She is only eighteen months old, and I am afraid that some superstitious creature has killed her for one of her feet."

Fred Fox turned the snapshot over and put it in his pocket. "Has this bunny got a throb?" he asked.

"Yes," said old Mrs. Rabbit. "Franz Frog, repulsive owner of the notorious Lily Pad Night Club."

Fred Fox leaped to his feet. "Come on, Grandma," he said, "and don't step on your ears. We got to move fast."

134

On the way to the Lily Pad Night Club, old Mrs. Rabbit scampered so fast that Fred Fox had all he could do to keep up with her. "Daphne is my great-great-great-great-great-grand-daughter, if my memory serves," said old Mrs. Rabbit. "I have thirty-nine thousand descendants."

"This isn't going to be easy," said Fred Fox. "Maybe you should have gone to a magician with a hat."

"But she is the only one named Daphne," said old Mrs. Rabbit, "and she lived alone with me on my great carrot farm."

They came to a broad brook. "Skip it!" said Fred Fox.

"Keep a civil tongue in your head, young man," snapped old Mrs. Rabbit.

Just as they got to the Lily Pad, a dandelion clock struck twelve noon. Fred Fox pushed the button on the great green door, on which was painted a white water lily. The door opened an eighth of an inch, and Ben Rat peered out. "Beat it," he said, but Fred Fox shoved the door open, and old Mrs. Rabbit followed him into a cool green hallway, softly but restlessly lighted by thousands of fireflies imprisoned in the hollow crystal pendants of an enormous chandelier. At the right there was a flight of green-carpeted stairs, and at the bottom of the steps the door to the cloakroom. Straight ahead, at the end of the long hallway, was the cool green door to Franz Frog's office.

"Beat it," said Ben Rat again.

"Talk nice," said Fred Fox, "or I'll seal your house up with tin. Where's the Croaker?"

"Once a gumpaw, always a gumpaw," grumbled Ben Rat. "He's in his office."

"With Daphne?"

"Who's Daphne?" asked Ben Rat.

"My great-great-great-great-great-granddaughter," said old Mrs. Rabbit.

"Nobody's that great," snarled Ben Rat.

Fred Fox opened the cool green door and went into Franz Frog's office, followed by old Mrs. Rabbit and Ben Rat. The owner of the Lily Pad sat behind his desk, wearing a green suit, green shirt, green tie, green socks, and green shoes. He had an emerald tiepin and seven emerald rings. "Whong you wong, Fonnxx?" he rumbled in a cold, green, cavernous voice. His eyes bulged and his throat began to swell ominously.

"He's going to croak," explained Ben Rat.

"Nuts," said Fred Fox. "He'll outlive all of us."

"Glunk," croaked Franz Frog.

Ben Rat glared at Fred Fox. "You oughta go on the stage," he snarled.

"Where's Daphne?" demanded Fred Fox.

"Hoong Dangneng?" asked Franz Frog.

"Your bunny friend," said Fred Fox.

"Nawng," said Franz Frog.

Fred Fox picked up a cello in a corner and put it down. It was too light to contain a rabbit. The front-door bell rang. "I'll get it," said Fred Fox. It was Oliver (Hoot) Owl, a notorious fly-by-night. "What're you doing up at this hour, Hoot?" asked Fred Fox.

"I'm trying to blind myself, so I'll confess," said Hoot Owl testily.

"Confess to what?" snapped Fred Fox.

"What can't you solve?" asked Hoot Owl.

"The disappearance of Daphne," said Fred Fox.

"Who's Daphne?" asked Hoot Owl.

Franz Frog hopped out of his office into the hall. Ben Rat and old Mrs. Rabbit followed him.

Down the steps from the second floor came Sherman Stork, carrying a white muffler or something and grinning foolishly.

"Well, bless my soul!" said Fred Fox. "If it isn't old mid-husband himself! What did you do with Daphne?"

"Who's Daphne?" asked Sherman Stork.

"Fox thinks somebody killed Daphne Rabbit," said Ben Rat.

"Fonnxx cung brong," rumbled Franz Frog.

"I *could* be wrong," said Fred Fox, "but I'm not." He pulled open the cloakroom door at the bottom of the steps, and the dead body of a female white rabbit toppled furrily on to the cool green carpet. Her head had been bashed in by a heavy blunt instrument.

"Daphne!" screamed old Mrs. Rabbit, bursting into tears.

"I can't see a thing," said Hoot Owl.

"It's a dead white rabbit," said Ben Rat. "Anybody can see that. You're dumb."

"I'm wise!" said Hoot Owl indignantly. "I know everything."

"Jeeng Crine," moaned Franz Frog. He stared up at the chandelier, his eyes bulging and his mammoth mouth gaping open. All the fireflies were frightened and went out.

The cool green hallway became pitch dark. There was a shriek in the black and a feathery "plump." The fireflies lighted up to see what had happened. Hoot Owl lay dead on the cool green carpet, his head bashed in by a heavy blunt instrument. Ben Rat, Franz Frog, Sherman Stork, old Mrs. Rabbit, and Fred Fox stared at Hoot Owl. Over the cool green carpet crawled a warm red stain, whose source was the body of Hoot Owl. He lay like a feather duster.

"Murder!" squealed old Mrs. Rabbit.

"Nobody leaves this hallway!" snapped Fred Fox. "There's a killer loose in this club!"

"I am not used to death," said Sherman Stork.

"Roong!" groaned Franz Frog.

"He says he's ruined," said Ben Rat, but Fred Fox wasn't listening. He was looking for a heavy blunt instrument. There wasn't any.

"Search them!" cried old Mrs. Rabbit. "Somebody has a sap, or a sock full of sand, or something!"

"Yeh," said Fred Fox. "Ben Rat is a sap—maybe someone swung him by his tail."

"You oughta go on the stage," snarled Ben Rat.

Fred Fox searched the suspects, but he found no concealed weapon. "You could have strangled them with that muffler," Fred Fox told Sherman Stork.

"But they were not strangled," said Sherman Stork.

Fred Fox turned to Ben Rat. "You could have bitten them to death with your ugly teeth," he said.

"But they weren't bitten to death," said Ben Rat.

Fred Fox stared at Franz Frog. "You could have scared them to death with your ugly face," he said.

"Bung wung screng ta deng," said Franz Frog.

"You're right," admitted Fred Fox. "They weren't. Where's old Mrs. Rabbit?" he asked suddenly.

"I'm hiding in here," called old Mrs. Rabbit from the cloakroom. "I'm frightened."

Fred Fox got her out of the cool green sanctuary and went in himself. It was dark. He groped around on the cool green carpet. He didn't know what he was looking for, but he found it, a small object lying in a far corner. He put it in his pocket and came out of the cloakroom.

"What'd you find, shamus?" asked Ben Rat apprehensively.

"Exhibit A," said Fred Fox casually.

"Sahng plang keeng," moaned Franz Frog.

"He says somebody's playing for keeps," said Ben Rat.

"He can say that again," said Fred Fox as the front door was flung open and Inspector Mastiff trotted in, followed by Sergeant Dachshund.

"Well, well, look who's muzzling in," said Fred Fox.

"What have we got here?" barked Inspector Mastiff.

"I hate a private nose," said Sergeant Dachshund.

Fred Fox grinned at him. "What happened to your legs from the knees down, sport?" he asked.

"Drop dead," snarled Sergeant Dachshund.

"Quiet, both of you!" snapped Inspector Mastiff. "I know Ollie Owl, but who's the twenty-dollar Easter present from Schrafft's?" He turned on Fred Fox. "If this bunny's head comes off and she's filled with candy, I'll have your badge, Fox," he growled.

"She's real, Inspector," said Fred Fox. "Real dead, too. How did you pick up the scent?"

Inspector Mastiff howled. "The Sergeant thought he smelt a rat at the Lily Club," he said. "Wrong again, as usual. Who's this dead rabbit?"

"She's my great-great-great-great-great-granddaughter," sobbed old Mrs. Rabbit.

Fred Fox lighted a cigarette. "Oh, no, she isn't, sweetheart," he said coolly. "You are *her* great-great-great-great-great-grand-daughter." Pink lightning flared in the live white rabbit's eyes. "You killed the old lady, so you could take over her carrot farm," continued Fred Fox, "and then you killed Hoot Owl."

"I'll kill you, too, shamus!" shrieked Daphne Rabbit.

"Put the cuffs on her, Sergeant," barked Inspector Mastiff. Sergeant Dachshund put a pair of handcuffs on the front legs of the dead rabbit. "Not *her*, you dumb kraut!" yelped Inspector Mastiff. It was too late. Daphne Rabbit had jumped through a windowpane and run away, with the Sergeant in hot pursuit.

"All white rabbits look alike to me," growled Inspector Mastiff. "How could you tell them apart—from their ears?"

"No," said Fred Fox. "From their years. The white rabbit that called on me darn near beat me to the Lily Pad, and no old woman can do that."

"Don't brag," said Inspector Mastiff. "Spryness isn't enough. What else?"

"She understood expressions an old rabbit doesn't know," said Fred Fox, "like 'hop the hutch' and 'throb' and 'skip it' and 'sap.'"

"You can't hang a rabbit for her vocabulary," said Inspector Mastiff. "Come again."

Fred Fox pulled the snapshot out of his pocket. "The white rabbit who called on me told me Daphne was eighteen months old," he said, "but read what it says on the back of this picture."

Inspector Mastiff took the snapshot, turned it over, and read, "'Daphne on her second birthday.'"

"Yes," said Fred Fox. "Daphne knocked six months off her age. You see, Inspector, she couldn't read the writing on the snapshot, because those weren't her spectacles she was wearing."

"Now wait a minute," growled Inspector Mastiff. "Why did she kill Hoot Owl?"

"Elementary, my dear Mastiff," said Fred Fox. "Hoot Owl lived in an oak tree, and she was afraid he saw her burrowing into the club last night, dragging Grandma. She heard Hoot Owl say, 'I'm wise. I know everything,' and so she killed him."

"What with?" demanded the Inspector.

"Her right hind foot," said Fred Fox. "I was looking for a concealed weapon, and all the time she was carrying her heavy blunt instrument openly."

"Well, what do you know!" exclaimed Inspector Mastiff. "Do you think Hoot Owl really saw her?"

"Could be," said Fred Fox. "I happen to think he was bragging about his wisdom in general and not about a particular piece of information, but your guess is as good as mine."

"What did you pick up in the cloakroom?" squeaked Ben Rat.

"The final strand in the rope that will hang Daphne," said Fred Fox. "I knew she didn't go in there to hide. She went in there to look for something she lost last night. If she'd been frightened, she would have hidden when the flies went out, but she went in there after the flies lighted up again."

"That adds up," said Inspector Mastiff grudgingly. "What was it she was looking for?"

"Well," said Fred Fox, "she heard something drop in the dark when she dragged Grandma in there last night and she thought it was a button, or a buckle, or a bead, or a bangle, or a brooch that would incriminate her. That's why she rang me in on the case. She couldn't come here alone to look for it."

"Well, what was it, Fox?" snapped Instructor Mastiff.

"A carrot," said Fred Fox, and he took it out of his pocket, "probably fell out of old Mrs. Rabbit's reticule, if you like irony."

"One more question," said Inspector Mastiff. "Why plant the body in the Lily Pad?"

"Easy," said Fred Fox. "She wanted to throw suspicion on the Croaker, a well-known lady-killer."

"Nawng," rumbled Franz Frog.

"Well, there it is, Inspector," said Fred Fox, "all wrapped up for you and tied with ribbons."

Ben Rat disappeared into a wall. Franz Frog hopped back to his office.

"Mercy!" cried Sherman Stork. "I'm late for an appointment!" He flew to the front door and opened it.

There stood Daphne Rabbit, holding the unconscious form of Sergeant Dachshund. "I give up," she said. "I surrender."

"Is he dead?" asked Inspector Mastiff hopefully.

"No," said Daphne Rabbit. "He fainted."

"I never have any luck," growled Inspector Mastiff.

Fred Fox leaned over and pointed to Daphne's right hind foot. "Owl feathers," he said. "She's all yours, Inspector."

"Thanks, Fox," said Inspector Mastiff. "I'll throw something your way some day."

"Make it a nice, plump Plymouth Rock pullet," said Fred Fox, and he sauntered out of the Lily Pad.

Back in his office, Fred Fox dictated his report on the White Rabbit Caper to his secretary, Lura Fox. "Period. End of report," he said finally, toying with the emerald stickpin he had taken from Franz Frog's green necktie when the fireflies went out.

"Is she pretty?" asked Lura Fox.

"Daphne? Quite a dish," said Fred Fox, "but I like my rabbits stewed, and I'm afraid little Daphne is going to fry."

"But she's so young, Fred!" cried Lura Fox. "Only eighteen months!"

"You weren't listening," said Fred Fox.

"How did you know she wasn't interested in Franz Frog?" asked Lura Fox.

"Simple," said Fred Fox. "Wrong species."

"What became of the candy, Fred?" asked Lura Fox.

Fred Fox stared at her. "What candy?" he asked blankly.

Lura Fox suddenly burst into tears. "She was so soft, and warm, and cuddly, Fred," she wailed.

Fred Fox filled a glass with rye, drank it slowly, set down the glass, and sighed grimly. "Sour racket," he said.

Afternoon of a Playwright

I CALLED the other afternoon, at the laudanum hour, upon Bernard Hudley, the dramatist, and found him, to my astonishment, somewhat less despondent than he had been on my previous visit some months before. "What's the matter?" I asked anxiously. "Can I do anything to depress you?"

He didn't answer, but sat staring at a blank piece of paper in his typewriter.

"I am trying to outline a drawing-room comedy of horror," he said finally, "but a note of hope, even of decency, keeps creeping into it."

"That's too bad," I told him. "What's the time of the play? Maybe that's where the fault lies."

He pulled the paper out of the typewriter, tore off a piece, and began chewing it. "It's set in Tanganyika, 600,000 years ago," he said. "I want to show that mankind came to an end that year, and that we do not now, in fact, exist. But 600,000 years ago doesn't seem gloomy enough, somehow."

I thought about his problem for a moment, and then said, "I think I see what's the matter. Why don't you make it 598,000 B.C.?"

His eyes lighted gloomily. "You may have something ghastly there," he admitted.

"But I don't think they had drawing rooms in those years," I told him.

"This is not an ordinary drawing room," he snapped. "I call it a drawing and quartering room."

"Now you're being your old self again," I said. "Who are you using for characters?"

"Devils and demons," he said, "all of them possessed by human beings. I like that part of it all right, but there's nowhere to go from there except up, and you know how I hate up. The first act is terrifying enough to suit me, but I don't know what to do about the second act yet."

I lit the wrong end of a filter cigarette and handed it to him. "What's the scene of the second act?" I asked.

"A combination madhouse and brothel," he said. "A convention of clergymen has taken it over for the weekend. You see what I mean by the note of hope creeping in?"

"I do indeed," I said. I got up, walked to the bar in the corner of the room and picked up a bottle.

"Not that one," he said quickly. "That's poisoned. Take the one on the right." I knew Hudley well enough to figure that the bottle on the right was the poisoned one, so I poured a drink from the one I had selected.

"Damn your intuition!" he snarled. "You're worse than Myra. She has lost her sense of smell completely, but I still can't fool her about those bottles." His wife, Myra, walked into the room at that moment, wearing dark glasses and showing her lower teeth.

"Bad afternoon," I said. "I hope you're feeling awful."

"Bad afternoon," she said, and then to her husband, "It's time for you not to take your thyroid pills." He didn't say anything.

"You two have been married for three weeks now," I said. "What's the matter?"

"Oh, we have tried everything," she said, "but something always goes right. You know how things are nowadays."

He looked gloomier than ever. "Now Myra's having an affair with a police lieutenant," he told me. "She always picks the wrong man, someone that can't run away with her."

Myra laughed—at least I think it was laughter, although it sounded more like pieces of iron falling into a bathtub. "Bernard wants the girl next door, but she's too old for him," Myra said. "She's nine."

"And not getting any younger, I suppose," I put in, unable to think of anything else.

Suddenly, from somewhere in the house, there were two pistol shots in rapid succession.

"This house is the noisiest place this side of hell," growled Hudley.

"Who's shooting who?" I asked as casually as I could.

Myra took a drink straight from the bottle from which I had poured mine. "Either my sister has shot her lover, or vice versa," she said.

"Well, don't go and find out," her husband croaked. "I've no time for details. Maybe I ought to go back to that play about the Wright brothers at Kitty Hawk."

"Why did you drop it in the first place?" I asked him.

"It got cheerful on me," he said. "I call them the Fright brothers and made the setting Night Hawk. They both crack up on their first flight, and that prevents the development of the airplane."

"I see," I said. "It *is* cheerful. That would, of course, have prevented the invention of the modern bomber and all the other deadly warplanes."

Myra sat down in a chair and began reading a copy of a magazine called *Horrible Love Tales*. I began to feel, for some reason, a little nervous. "What became of the play you were working on last year called *The Explosion?*" I asked.

"Couldn't find a producer," Hudley grumbled. "They all said it needed development, that it was too short."

"What did they mean?" I asked.

Hudley ate another piece of paper, and said, "The curtain goes up on an empty stage, and before any character appears the whole damn set blows up. It seemed gruesome enough to me, and definitely unique."

Myra gave her iron laugh again. "Gruesome, hell!" she said. "Most hilarious play he ever wrote. You don't see anybody get killed, and, furthermore, the audience could leave the theater and go to the nearest bar and have a good time."

"There ought to be a law against people having a good time," I said and stood up. "Bad bye." I bowed to both of them, and backed out of the room toward the front door, so that I wouldn't be stabbed or shot in the back.

As I went down the front steps of the Hudley house, a man in the uniform of a police lieutenant came up to me. It was Myra's lover. "Somebody reported hearing shots in there," he said, and added, hopefully, "Did she get Hudley this time?"

"No," I told him. "Mrs. Hudley's sister shot her lover, or he shot her. We were pretty busy discussing modern plays and nobody had time to look."

"You better come back with me, Mac," he said. "Maybe I can pin it on you. I love to pin crimes on the wrong man."

"You ought to be a playwright," I told him. "You seem to have a natural talent for the modern drama."

He led me back into the house and, when we got to the living room, both Hudley and Myra were lying on the floor. They had bored each other to death in my absence.

"Always business." The lieutenant laughed horribly. "I never have a cheerless moment." He went to the telephone and called the police station. "Let me have Police Inspector Rawlings," he said, and then, "What do you mean, he isn't there? Gone out of town? How long will he be gone? Two days? Good."

"You said good," I told him. "That's bad."

"We all make mistakes," he snarled, and he dialed another number. "Is this Inspector Rawlings' house?" he said into the receiver. "Let me talk to Mrs. Rawlings." There was a pause, and then he said, "Eleanor? I've just found out your husband is out of town for two days. Put on something uncomfortable. I'll be right over." He hung up and started out of the room. As he stepped over what I had thought was Hudley's dead body, the playwright deftly tripped him, causing him to fall and break his neck.

"Somebody will have to call Mrs. Rawlings," I said, and Myra sat up, with the eager look of a little girl at a circus. "I'll handle that," she said brightly, as she went to the phone.

"I think I know what to do with the clergymen in the brothel," I told Hudley.

"It better be awful," he snarled.

"It is," I said. "Why not make them all insane? Then you could call the play *Too Many Kooks Spoil the Brothel.*"

Hudley and Myra pulled guns on me at the same moment, but before they could fire their little son walked into the room and got both of them with a double-barreled shotgun. "Dad wouldn't let me have the car tonight," he explained. "And Mom wanted me to do my homework." Suddenly he drew a knife and threw it at me.

"Wake up! Wake up!" said my wife's voice, from the next bed. I woke up groggily.

"What became of all the bodies?" I mumbled.

"I don't know and I don't care," my wife said, "but you were yelling in your sleep. Don't you *ever* have any pleasant dreams?" I glanced at my wristwatch. It was a quarter after six. I didn't know whether to get up, or try to go back to sleep. It was nightmare either way.

"You want a drink?" I asked my wife, but she was asleep again. I dressed and went downstairs, and poured myself a stiff drink of straight whiskey. I raised the glass and said to the vanished figures of my nightmare, "There's no place to go but down." Then I downed the drink. An hour later I was feeling much worse. I had picked the wrong bottle, the unpoisoned one.

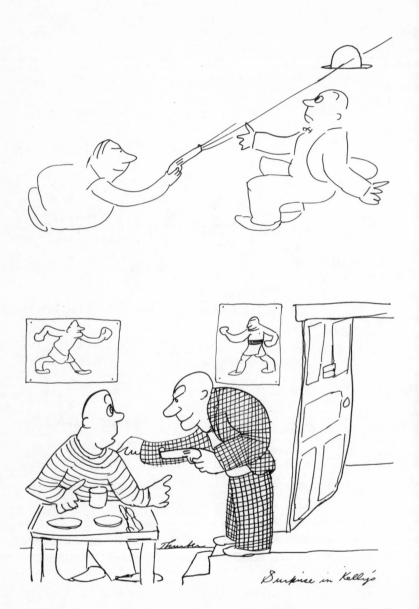

Surprise in Kelly's

A Friend to Alexander

I HAVE TAKEN TO DREAMING about Aaron Burr every night,"
Andrews said.

"What for?" said Mrs. Andrews.

"How do I know what for?" Andrews snarled. "What for, the
woman says."

Mrs. Andrews did not flare up; she simply looked at her
husband as he lay on the chaise longue in her bedroom in his
heavy blue dressing gown, smoking a cigarette. Although he had
just got out of bed, he looked haggard and tired. He kept biting
his lower lip between puffs.

"Aaron Burr is a funny person to be dreaming about
nowadays—I mean with all the countries in the world threatening
each other. I wish you would go and see Dr. Fox," said Mrs.
Andrews, taking her thumb from between the pages of her
mystery novel and tossing the book toward the foot of her bed.
She sat up straighter against her pillow. "Maybe haliver oil or B_1
is what you need," she said. "B_1 does wonders for people. I don't
see why you see *him* in your dreams. *Where* do you see him?"

"Oh, places; in Washington Square or Bowling Green or on
Broadway. I'll be talking to a woman in a victoria, a woman
holding a white lace parasol, and suddenly there will be Burr,

bowing and smiling and smelling like a carnation, telling his stories about France and getting off his insults."

Mrs. Andrews lighted a cigarette, although she rarely smoked until after lunch. "Who is the woman in the victoria?" she asked.

"What? How do I know? You know about people in dreams, don't you? They are nobody at all, or everybody."

"You see Aaron Burr plainly enough, though. I mean he isn't nobody or everybody."

"All right, all right," said Andrews. "You have me there. But I don't know who the woman is, and I don't care. Maybe it's Madame Jumel or Mittens Willett or a girl I knew in high school. That's not important."

"Who is Mittens Willett?" asked Mrs. Andrews.

"She was a famous New York actress in her day, fifty years ago or so. She's buried in an old cemetery on Second Avenue."

"That's very sad," said Mrs. Andrews.

"Why is it?" demanded Andrews, who was now pacing up and down the deep-red carpet.

"I mean she probably died young," said Mrs. Andrews. "Almost all women did in those days."

Andrews ignored her and walked over to a window and looked out at a neat, bleak street in the Fifties. "He's a vile, cynical cad," said Andrews, suddenly turning away from the window. "I was standing talking to Alexander Hamilton when Burr stepped up and slapped him in the face. When I looked at Hamilton, who do you suppose he was?"

"I don't know," said Mrs. Andrews. "Who was he?"

"He was my brother, the one I've told you about, the one who was killed by that drunkard in the cemetery."

Mrs. Andrews had never got that story straight and she didn't want to go into it again now; the facts in the tragic case and her way of getting them mixed up always drove Andrews into a white-faced fury. "I don't think we ought to dwell on your nightmare," said Mrs. Andrews. "I think we ought to get out more. We could go to the country for weekends."

Andrews wasn't listening; he was back at the window, staring out into the street again.

"I wish he'd go back to France and stay there," Andrews snapped out suddenly the next morning at breakfast.

"Who, dear?" said his wife. "Oh, you mean Aaron Burr. Did you dream about him again? I don't see why you dream about him all the time. Don't you think you ought to take some Luminal?"

"No," said Andrews. "I don't know. Last night he kept shoving Alexander around."

"Alexander?"

"Hamilton. God knows I'm familiar enough with him to call him by his first name. He hides behind my coattails every night, or tries to."

"I was thinking we might go to the Old Drovers' Inn this weekend," said Mrs. Andrews. "You like it there."

"Hamilton has become not only my brother Walter but practically every other guy I have ever liked," said Andrews. "That's natural."

"Of course it is," she said. They got up from the table. "I do wish you'd go to Dr. Fox."

"I'm going to the zoo," he said, "and feed popcorn to the rhinoceros. That makes things seem right, for a little while, anyway."

It was two nights later at five o'clock in the morning that Andrews bumbled into his wife's bedroom in pajamas and bare feet, his hair in his eyes, his eyes wild. "He got him!" he croaked. "He got him! The bastard got him. Alexander fired into the air, he fired in the air and smiled at him, just like Walter, and that fiend from hell took deliberate aim—I saw him—I saw him take deliberate aim—he killed him in cold blood, the foul scum!"

Mrs. Andrews, not quite awake, was fumbling in the box containing the Nembutal while her husband ranted on. She made him take two of the little capsules, between his sobs.

Andrews didn't want to go to see Dr. Fox but he went to humor his wife. Dr. Fox leaned back in his swivel chair behind his desk and looked at Andrews. "Now, just what seems to be the trouble?" he asked.

"Nothing seems to be the trouble," said Andrews.

The doctor looked at Mrs. Andrews. "He has nightmares," she said.

"You look a little underweight, perhaps," said the doctor. "Are you eating well, getting enough exercise?"

"I'm not underweight," said Andrews. "I eat the way I always have and get the same exercise."

At this, Mrs. Andrews sat straighter in her chair and began to talk, while her husband lighted a cigarette. "You see, I think he's worried about something," she said, "because he always has this same dream. It's about his brother Walter, who was killed in a cemetery by a drunken man, only it isn't *really* about him."

The doctor did the best he could with this information. He cleared his throat, tapped on the glass top of his desk with the fingers of his right hand, and said, "Very few people are actually *killed* in cemeteries." Andrews stared at the doctor coldly and said nothing. "I wonder if you would mind stepping into the next room," the doctor said to him.

"Well, I hope you're satisfied," Andrews snapped at his wife as they left the doctor's office a half hour later. "You heard what he said. There's nothing the matter with me at all."

"I'm glad your heart is so fine," she told him. "He said it was fine, you know."

"Sure," said Andrews. "It's fine. Everything's fine." They got into a cab and drove home in silence.

"I was just thinking," said Mrs. Andrews, as the cab stopped in front of their apartment building, "I was just thinking that now that Alexander Hamilton is dead, you won't see anything more of Aaron Burr." The cabdriver, who was handing Andrews change for a dollar bill, dropped a quarter on the floor.

Mrs. Andrews was wrong. Aaron Burr did not depart from her husband's dreams. Andrews said nothing about it for several mornings, but she could tell. He brooded over his breakfast, did not answer any of her questions, and jumped in his chair if she dropped a knife or spoon. "Are you still dreaming about that man?" she asked him finally.

"I wish I hadn't told you about it," he said. "Forget it, will you?"

"I can't forget it with you going on this way," she said. "I think you ought to see a psychiatrist. What does he do now?"

"What does who do now?" Andrews asked.

"Aaron Burr," she said. "I don't see why he keeps coming into your dreams now."

Andrews finished his coffee and stood up. "He goes around bragging that he did it with his eyes closed," he snarled. "He says he didn't even look. He claims he can hit the ace of spades at thirty paces blindfolded. Furthermore, since you asked what he does, he jostles me at parties now."

Mrs. Andrews stood up too and put her hand on her husband's shoulder. "I think you should stay out of this, Harry," she said. "It wasn't any business of yours, anyway, and it happened so long ago."

"I'm not getting into anything," said Andrews, his voice rising to a shout. "It's getting into me. Can't you see that?"

"I see that I've got to get you away from here," she said. "Maybe if you slept someplace else for a few nights, you wouldn't dream about him any more. Let's go to the country tomorrow. Let's go to the Lime Rock Lodge."

Andrews stood for a long while without answering her. "Why can't we go and visit the Crowleys?" he said finally. "They live in the country. Bob has a pistol and we could do a little target shooting."

"What do you want to shoot a pistol for?" she asked quickly. "I should think you'd want to get away from that."

"Yeh," he said, "sure," and there was a far-off look in his eyes. "Sure."

When they drove into the driveway of the Crowleys' house, several miles north of New Milford, late the next afternoon, Andrews was whistling "Bye-Bye Blackbird." Mrs. Andrews sighed contentedly and then, as her husband stopped the car, she began looking around wildly. "My bag!" she cried. "Did I forget to bring my bag?" He laughed his old, normal laugh for the first time in many days as he found the bag and handed it to her, and then, for the first time in many days, he leaned over and kissed her.

The Crowleys came out of the house and engulfed their guests in questions and exclamations. "How you been?" said Bob Crowley to Andrews, heartily putting an arm around his shoulder.

"Never better," said Andrews, "never better. Boy, is it good to be here!"

They were swept into the house to a shakerful of Bob Crowley's icy Martinis. Mrs. Andrews stole a happy glance over the edge of her glass at her husband's relaxed face.

When Mrs. Andrews awoke the next morning, her husband lay rigidly on his back in the bed next to hers, staring at the ceiling. "Oh, God," said Mrs. Andrews.

Andrews didn't move his head. "One Henry Andrews, an architect," he said suddenly in a mocking tone. "One Henry Andrews, an architect."

"What's the matter, Harry?" she asked. "Why don't you go back to sleep? It's only eight o'clock."

"That's what he calls me!" shouted Andrews. "'One Henry Andrews, an architect,' he keeps saying in his nasty little sneering voice. 'One Henry Andrews, an architect.'"

"Please don't yell!" said Mrs. Andrews. "You'll wake the whole house. It's early. People want to sleep."

Andrews lowered his voice a little. "I'm beneath him," he snarled. "I'm just anybody. I'm a man in a gray suit. 'Be on your good behavior, my good man,' he says to me, 'or I shall have one of my lackeys give you a taste of the riding crop.'"

Mrs. Andrews sat up in bed. "Why should he say that to you?" she asked. "He wasn't such a great man, was he? I mean, didn't he try to sell Louisiana to the French, or something, behind Washington's back?"

"He was a scoundrel," said Andrews, "but a very brilliant mind."

Mrs. Andrews lay down again. "I was in hopes you weren't going to dream about him any more," she said. "I thought if I brought you up here—"

"It's him or me," said Andrews grimly. "I can't stand this forever."

"Neither can I," Mrs. Andrews said, and there was a hint of tears in her voice.

Andrews and his host spent most of the afternoon, as Mrs. Andrews had expected, shooting at targets on the edge of the wood behind the Crowley studio. After the first few rounds, Andrews surprised Crowley by standing with his back to the huge hulk of dead tree trunk on which the target was nailed, walking thirty paces ahead in a stiff-legged, stern-faced manner, with his revolver held at arm's length above his head, then turning suddenly and firing.

Crowley dropped to the ground, uninjured but scared. "What the hell's the big idea, Harry?" he yelled.

Andrews didn't say anything, but started to walk back to the tree again. Once more he stood with his back to the target and began stepping off the thirty paces.

"I think they kept their arm hanging straight down," Bob called to him. "I don't think they stuck it up in the air."

Andrews, still counting to himself, lowered his arm, and this time, as he turned at the thirtieth step, he whirled and fired from his hip, three times in rapid succession.

"Hey!" said Crowley.

Two of the shots missed the tree but the last one hit it, about two feet under the target. Crowley looked at his house guest oddly as Andrews began to walk back to the tree again, without a word, his lips tight, his eyes bright, his breath coming fast.

"What the hell?" Crowley said to himself. "Look, it's my turn," he called, but Andrews turned, then stalked ahead, unheeding. This time when he wheeled and fired, his eyes were closed.

"Good God Almighty, man!" said Crowley from the grass, where he lay flat on his stomach. "Hey, give me that gun, will you?" he demanded, getting to his feet.

Andrews let him take it. "I need a lot more practice, I guess," he said.

"Not with me standing around," said Crowley. "Come on, let's go back to the house and shake up a drink. I've got the jumps."

"I need a lot more practice," said Andrews again.

He got his practice next morning just as the sun came up and the light was hard and the air was cold. He had crawled softly out of bed, dressed silently, and crept out of the room. He knew where Crowley kept the target pistol and the cartridges. There would be a target on the tree trunk, just as high as a man's heart. Mrs. Andrews heard the shots first and sat sharply upright in bed, crying "Harry!" almost before she was awake. Then she heard more shots. She got up, put on a dressing gown, and went to the Crowley's door. She heard them moving about in their room. Alice opened the door and stepped out into the hall when Mrs. Andrews knocked. "Is Harry all right?" asked Mrs. Andrews. "Where is he? What is he doing?"

"He's out shooting behind the studio, Bob says," Alice told her. "Bob'll go out and get him. Maybe he had a nightmare, or walked in his sleep."

"No," said Mrs. Andrews, "he never walks in his sleep. He's awake."

"Let's go down and put on some coffee," said Alice. "He'll need some."

Crowley came out of the bedroom and joined the women in the hallway. "I'll need some too," he said. "Good morning, Bess. I'll bring him back. What the hell's the matter with him, anyway?" He was down the stairs and gone before she could answer. She was glad of that.

"Come on," said Alice, taking her arm. They went down to the kitchen.

Mrs. Crowley found the butler in the kitchen, just standing there. "It's all right, Madison," she said. "You go back to bed. Tell Clotheta it's all right. Mr. Andrews is just shooting a little. He couldn't sleep."

"Yes, Ma'am," mumbled Madison, and went back to tell his wife that they said it was all right.

"It can't be right," said Clotheta, "shootin' pistols at this time of night."

"Hush up," Madison told her. He was shivering as he climbed back into bed.

"I wish dat man would go 'way from heah," grumbled Clotheta. "He's got a bad look to his eyes."

Andrews brightened Clotheta's life by going away late that afternoon. When he and his wife got in their car and drove off, the Crowleys slumped into chairs and looked at each other and said, "Well." Crowley got up finally to mix a drink. "What do you think is the matter with Harry?" he asked.

"I don't know," said his wife. "It's what Clotheta would call the shoots, I suppose."

"He said a funny thing when I went out and got him this morning," Crowley told her.

"I could stand a funny thing," she said.

"I asked him what the hell he was doing there in that freezing air with only his pants and shirt and shoes on. 'I'll get him one of these nights,' he said."

"Why don't you sleep in my room tonight?" Mrs. Andrews asked her husband as he finished his Scotch-and-water nightcap.

"You'd keep shaking me all night to keep me awake," he said. "You're afraid to let me meet him. Why do you always think everybody else is better than I am? I can outshoot him the best day he ever lived. Furthermore, I have a modern pistol. He has to use an old-fashioned single-shot muzzle-loader." Andrews laughed nastily.

"Is that quite fair?" his wife asked after a moment of thoughtful silence.

He jumped up from his chair. "What do I care if it's fair or not?" he snarled.

She got up too. "Don't be mad with me, Harry," she said. There were tears in her eyes.

"I'm sorry, darling," he said, taking her in his arms.

"I'm very unhappy," she sobbed.

"I'm sorry, darling," he said again. "Don't you worry about me. I'll be all right. I'll be fine." She was crying too wildly to say anything more.

When she kissed him good night later on she knew it was really goodbye. Women have a way of telling when you aren't coming back.

"Extraordinary," said Dr. Fox the next morning, letting Andrews' dead left hand fall back upon the bed. "His heart was as sound as a dollar when I examined him the other day. It has just stopped as if he had been shot."

Mrs. Andrews, through her tears, was looking at her dead husband's right hand. The three fingers next to the index finger were closed in stiffly on the palm, as if gripping the handle of a pistol. The taut thumb was doing its part to hold that invisible handle tightly and unwaveringly. But it was the index finger that Mrs. Andrews' eyes stayed on longest. It was only slightly curved inward, as if it were just about to press the trigger of the pistol. "Harry never even fired a shot," wailed Mrs. Andrews. "Aaron Burr killed him the way he killed Hamilton. Aaron Burr shot him through the heart. I knew he would. I knew he would."

Dr. Fox put an arm about the hysterical woman and led her from the room. "She is crazy," he said to himself. "Stark, raving crazy."

The Patient Bloodhound

I N MAY, 1937, a bloodhound who lived in Wapokoneta Falls, Ohio, was put on the trail of a man suspected of a certain crime. The bloodhound followed him to Akron, Cleveland, Buffalo, Syracuse, Rochester, Albany, and New York. The Westminster dog show was going on at the time but the bloodhound couldn't get to the garden because the man got on the first ship for Europe. The ship landed at Cherbourg and the bloodhound followed the man to Paris, Beauvais, Calais, Dover, London, Chester, Llandudno, Bettws-y-Coed, and Edinburgh, where the dog wasn't able to take in the international sheep trials. From Edinburgh, the bloodhound trailed the man to Liverpool, but since the man immediately got on a ship for New York, the dog didn't have a chance to explore the wonderful Liverpool smells.

In America again, the bloodhound traced the man to Teaneck, Tenafly, Nyack, and Peapack—where the dog didn't have time to run with the Peapack beagles. From Peapack the hound followed the man to Cincinnati, St. Louis, Kansas City, St. Louis, Cincinnati, Columbus, Akron, and finally back to Wapokoneta Falls. There the man was acquitted of the crime he had been followed for.

The bloodhound had developed fallen paw-pads and he was so worn out he could never again trail anything that was faster than a turtle. Furthermore, since he had gone through the world with his eyes and nose to the ground, he had missed all its beauty and excitement.

Moral: The paths of glory at least lead to the Grave, but the paths of duty may not get you Anywhere.

Cuttings

(Some excerpts on crime, writers, and crime writers)

Dashiell Hammett

ONE NIGHT nearly thirty years ago, in a legendary New York *boîte de nuit et des arts* called Tony's, I was taking part in a running literary gunfight that had begun with a derogatory or complimentary remark somebody made about something, when one of the participants, former Pinkerton man Dashiell Hammett, whose *The Maltese Falcon* had come out a couple of years before, suddenly startled all of us by announcing that his writing had been influenced by Henry James' novel *The Wings of the Dove*. Nothing surprises me any more, but I couldn't have been more surprised than if Humphrey Bogart, another frequenter of that old salon of wassail and debate, had proclaimed that his acting bore the deep impress of the histrionic art of Maude Adams.

I was unable, in a recent reinvestigation, to find many feathers of "The Dove" in the claws of "The Falcon," but there are a few "faint, far" (as James used to say) resemblances. In both novels, a fabulous fortune—jewels in "The Falcon," inherited millions in "The Dove"—shapes the destinies of the disenchanted central characters; James' designing woman Kate Croy, like Hammett's pistol-packing babe Brigid O'Shaughnessy, loses her lover, although James' Renunciation Scene is managed, as who should say, more exquisitely than Hammett's, in which Sam Spade speaks those sweetly sorrowful parting words: "You angel! Well, if you get a break you'll be out of San Quentin in twenty years and you can come back to me then." Whereupon he turns her over to the cops for the murder of his partner, Miles Archer (a good old Henry James name, that).

Some strong young literary excavator may one day dig up other parallels, but I suggest that he avoid trying to relate the character in "The Falcon" called Cairo to James' early intention to use Cairo, instead of Venice, as the major setting of his novel. That is simply, as who should not say, one of those rococo coincidences.

From "The Wings of Henry James,"
in *Lanterns and Lances*

E.B. "Andy" White

If it wasn't one thing it was another, at the *New Yorker*, and sometimes both. There was the day, twenty-five years ago, when two New York detectives called on Ross. They wanted to ask questions about, and then of, one E.B. White, a writer and, the dicks half suspected, the brain guy behind the daring robbery of a bank in Ardsley, New York, not far from Tarrytown. Andy at that time owned a Buick sedan, which he kept in a garage in Turtle Bay, on New York's Upper East Side; it had been stolen from the garage one night and used in the robbery by the bandits. After a wild chase by state cops the robbers had abandoned the automobile with a few bullet holes in it. The car was then taken to the state police barracks at Hawthorne. They wouldn't let White have it for almost a month.

Ross, who was always at ease with cops, in uniform or in plainclothes, had a wonderful time about it all. He said to the detectives on their first visit, "I think you're on the right track all right. White has been silent and brooding—he's definitely got something on his mind that's worrying the hell out of him." He took the men to White's office, grinning widely, made a big gesture with his right hand and said, "There's your man, officers."

"The detectives paid two or three visits to my office, which pleased Ross greatly," White wrote me. "They would sit around on my couch and just study me, occasionally asking a question when they could think of one. The question I loved was when one of them said: 'Say, how did you get into writing, anyway?' I replied that I had just drifted into it."

The walls of Andy's office interested the detectives a lot. They contained some cockeyed drawings of mine, and the back jacket of Max Eastman's book *The Enjoyment of Laughter*, which had a photograph of the handsome author laughing. I had taken a pencil and blacked out two of his fine even white teeth, drawn a lock of hair over his forehead, and given his eyes and eyebrows a demented look, the whole thing lending a tone of loony abandon to the office. Also, on one wall, Andy had written down the day and time of an appointment with his dentist, and above the date I had scrawled "*Der Tag*" and above the hour "*l'heure*." I don't know what the cops made of this piece of cryptic trilingualism, but they must have wondered and worried about it. Andy got the car back finally, and the detectives were smart enough in the end to realize that the man who had just drifted into writing had not drifted into bank robbery, too.

From "Up Popped the Devil,"
in *The Years With Ross*

James M. Cain

James M. Cain was a puzzle to Ross. "We called him Dizzy Jim," an old-timer told me recently. "You were Daffy Jim." It seemed that Cain liked to work on the floor where there was a lot of room, and used to put the Talk of the Town department together down there. He once lifted high the hearts of Andy and Katherine White, at a Thanksgiving Day dinner at his apartment, by putting the turkey, platter and all, on the floor and carving it, blandly going on with the story he was telling, and he told stories exceedingly well.

Jim wasn't at the *New Yorker* long, only a few months, but the memory of him has not dwindled there. When he got the hell out, he didn't want to see Ross or the *New Yorker* again, and I don't blame him for leaving any mention of it out of the piece about him in *Who's Who*.

In 1931 my daughter had about seven months to go before she was born when her mother and I bought a house a mile outside Sandy Hook, Connecticut, and Ross pretended to be frightened when he heard about my plans to live in the country. Timid, as usual, about taking up personal matters with a man face to face, he assigned Cain the task of trying to dissuade me from moving out of the city. Jim had approached the subject gingerly in my office, with only a couple of sentences that I recognized as bearing the stamp of a Ross panic, when he suddenly stood up and said, "This is none of my business, or Ross's either. I'm sorry I mentioned it. Live where you want to and the way you want to."

From "More Miracle Men,"
in *The Years With Ross*

Norman "Gus" Kuehner

Norman Kuehner got the biggest exclusive news story of his career one day in 1929. He had the title of assistant managing editor then, but he was still a police reporter at heart. Five days earlier, the body of an Ohio State coed named Theora Hix had been found on a rifle range five miles north of the city, and Kuehner had followed every line of the murder story in all three Columbus papers. A lot of evidence pointed at James H. Snook, professor of veterinary medicine at the university. The county prosecutor had been unable to break the suspect down, but every time Kuehner's phone rang, he was sure he was going to hear the news that Snook had confessed. He hoped to hell the story would break for the afternoon papers. It was a little past noon, on Kuehner's fateful day, when the *Dispatch* man at the police station phoned him and said, "Shelly just told me he's going to eat lunch at the usual place today. Made quite a point of it." Shelly was Wilson G. Shellenbarger, an old friend of Kuehner's, who had been a patrolman when young Gus covered the cop house, and was now chief of detectives. The "usual place" was a restaurant at Spring and High streets where Kuehner sometimes had lunch with Shellenbarger. He was excited, but he kept his voice low and casual as he said into the phone, "O.K., I'll wander over there," and hung up. He stuck some folded copy paper in his pocket and hurried to the restaurant.

When Shellenbarger showed up, he told Kuehner that Snook had confessed a few hours earlier but that the story was being held for the morning papers. He explained that William C. Howells, Columbus representative of the Cleveland *Plain Dealer*, had been allowed to visit Snook in his cell that morning, together with another newspaperman. Snook had repeated his confession to them, and Howells had agreed to take the stand at the trial, and corroborate the state's evidence, if the prosecutor would hold the story for the morning papers. Shellenbarger wanted to give his old friend Kuehner a break, and he did. He poured out all the facts of the case, including the details of the long and gaudy affair between the college girl and the professor, that led up to the murder. Half an hour later, Kuehner hurried back to his office with a dozen pages of notes and began to hammer out his story. He was about half finished when the county prosecutor's office phoned to announce that a conference of newspapermen would be held there at three o'clock that afternoon. Smallsreed was sent to represent the *Dispatch*, and told to stick close to the prosecutor until four o'clock. When he got back, at five minutes after four, with an official carbon of Snook's confession, he was handed a copy of the *Dispatch's* late-afternoon edition, which had just hit the street. Kuehner's long and vivid story, interspersed with photographs, covered the whole front page.

Kuehner's big story was unsigned, and there was no mention of Shellenbarger's part in it. It wasn't until two years later that Smallsreed found out who wrote the story and where it came from. Kuehner didn't get any glory at the time, but he had the deep satisfaction of knowing that he had scooped the world on one of the biggest murder stories of the century. The ex-police reporter of the Columbus *Dispatch* had had his greatest hour.

> From "Newspaperman—Head and Shoulders,"
> in *The Thurber Album*

James Thurber

Some fifteen years ago, our usually tranquil community was violently upset by the attempted murder of a woman. The State Police questioned us all. "What kind of an artist are you?" a detective asked me, and I must have looked guilty as hell. I finally said, "I refuse to answer that question on the ground that it might incriminate me."

> From "Such A Phrase As Drifts Through Dreams,"
> in *Lanterns and Lances*

Death Comes for the Dowager.

*"Well, you see, the story really goes back to when I was a teensy-weensy
little girl."*

"I'm Virgo with the moon in Aries, if that will help you any."

"Here! Here! There's a place for that, sir!"

"Have you seen my pistol, Honey-bun?"

"I'm wearing gloves because I don't want to leave any fingerprints around."

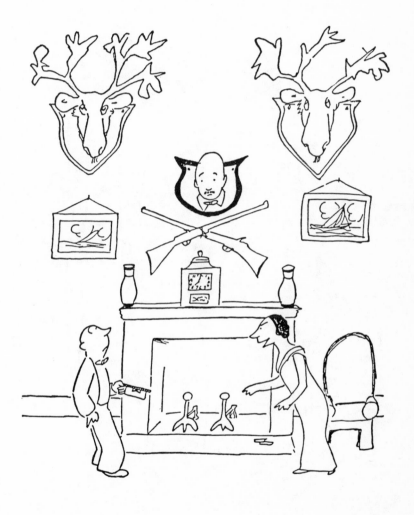

"Let me take your hat, Mr. Williams."

The Macbeth
Murder Mystery

I T WAS A STUPID MISTAKE to make," said the American woman I
had met at my hotel in the English lake country, "but it was on
the counter with the other Penguin books—the little sixpenny
ones, you know, with the paper covers—and I supposed of course
it was a detective story. All the others were detective stories. I'd
read all the others, so I bought this one without really looking at
it carefully. You can imagine how mad I was when I found it was
Shakespeare." I murmured something sympathetically. "I don't
see why the Penguin-books people had to get out Shakespeare's
plays in the same size and everything as the detective stories,"
went on my companion. "I think they have different-colored
jackets," I said. "Well, I didn't notice that," she said. "Anyway,
I got real comfy in bed that night and all ready to read a good
mystery story and here I had *The Tragedy of Macbeth*—a book for
high-school students. Like *Ivanhoe.*" "Or *Lorna Doone*," I said.
"Exactly," said the American lady. "And I was just crazy for a
good Agatha Christie, or something. Hercule Poirot is my favorite
detective." "Is he the rabbity one?" I asked. "Oh, no," said my
crime-fiction expert. "He's the Belgian one. You're thinking of
Mr. Pinkerton, the one that helps Inspector Bull. He's good,
too."

Over her second cup of tea my companion began to tell the plot of a detective story that had fooled her completely—it seems it was the old family doctor all the time. But I cut in on her. "Tell me," I said. "Did you read *Macbeth*?" "I *had* to read it," she said. "There wasn't a scrap of anything else to read in the whole room." "Did you like it?" I asked. "No, I did not," she said, decisively. "In the first place, I don't think for a moment that Macbeth did it." I looked at her blankly. "Did what?" I asked. "I don't think for a moment that he killed the King," she said. "I don't think the Macbeth woman was mixed up in it, either. You suspect them the most, of course, but those are the ones that are never guilty—or shouldn't be, anyway." "I'm afraid," I began, "that I—" "But don't you see?" said the American lady. "It would spoil everything if you could figure out right away who did it. Shakespeare was too smart for that. I've read that people never *have* figured out *Hamlet*, so it isn't likely Shakespeare would have made *Macbeth* as simple as it seems." I thought this over while I filled my pipe. "Who do you suspect?" I asked, suddenly. "Macduff," she said, promptly. "Good God!" I whispered, softly.

"Oh, Macduff did it, all right," said the murder specialist. "Hercule Poirot would have got him easily." "How did you figure it out?" I demanded. "Well," she said, "I didn't right away. At first I suspected Banquo. And then, of course, he was the second person killed. That was good right in there, that part. The person you suspect of the first murder should always be the second victim." "Is that so?" I murmured. "Oh, yes," said my informant. "They have to keep surprising you. Well, after the second murder I didn't know *who* the killer was for a while." "How about Malcolm and Donalbain, the King's sons?" I asked. "As I remember it, they fled right after the first murder. That looks suspicious." "Too suspicious," said the American lady. "Much too suspicious. When they flee, they're never guilty. You can count on that." "I believe," I said, "I'll have a brandy," and I summoned the waiter. My companion leaned toward me, her eyes bright, her teacup quivering. "Do you know who discovered Duncan's body?" she demanded. I said I was sorry, but I had forgotten. "Macduff discovers it," she said, slipping into the historical present. "Then he comes running downstairs and shouts, 'Confusion has broke open the Lord's anointed temple' and 'Sacrilegious murder has made his masterpiece' and on and on like that." The good lady tapped me on the knee. "All that stuff was *rehearsed*," she said. "You wouldn't say a lot of stuff like that, offhand, would you—if you had found a body?" She fixed me with a glittering eye. "I—" I began. "You're right!" she said. "You wouldn't! Unless you had practiced it in advance. 'My God, there's a body in here!' is what an innocent man would say." She sat back with a confident glare.

I thought for a while. "But what do you make of the Third Murderer?" I asked. "You know, the Third Murderer has puzzled *Macbeth* scholars for three hundred years." "That's because they never thought of Macduff," said the American lady. "It was Macduff, I'm certain. You couldn't have one of the victims murdered by two ordinary thugs—the murderer always has to be somebody important." "But what about the banquet scene?" I asked, after a moment. "How do you account for Macbeth's guilty actions there, when Banquo's ghost came in and sat in his chair?" The lady leaned forward and tapped me on the knee again. "There wasn't any ghost," she said. "A big, strong man like that doesn't go around seeing ghosts—especially in a brightly lighted banquet hall with dozens of people around. Macbeth was *shielding somebody!*" "Who was he shielding?" I asked. "Mrs. Macbeth, of course," she said. "He thought she did it and he was going to take the rap himself. The husband always does that when the wife is suspected." "But what," I demanded, "about the sleepwalking scene, then?" "The same thing, only the other way around," said my companion. "That time *she* was shielding *him*. She wasn't asleep at all. Do you remember where it says, 'Enter Lady Macbeth with a taper'?" "Yes," I said. "Well, people who walk in their sleep *never carry lights!*" said my fellow-traveller. "They have second sight. Did you ever hear of a sleepwalker carrying a light?" "No," I said, "I never did." "Well, then, she wasn't asleep. She was acting guilty to shield Macbeth." "I think," I said, "I'll have another brandy," and I called the waiter. When he brought it, I drank it rapidly and rose to go. "I believe," I said, "that you have got hold of something. Would you lend me that *Macbeth*? I'd like to look it over tonight. I don't feel, somehow, as if I'd ever really read it." "I'll get it for you," she said. "But you'll find that I am right."

I read the play over carefully that night, and the next morning, after breakfast, I sought out the American woman. She was on the putting green, and I came up behind her silently and took her arm. She gave an exclamation. "Could I see you alone?" I asked, in a low voice. She nodded cautiously and followed me to a secluded spot. "You've found out something?" she breathed. "I've found out," I said, triumphantly, "the name of the murderer!" "You mean it wasn't Macduff?" she said. "Macduff is as innocent of those murders," I said, "as Macbeth and the Macbeth woman." I opened the copy of the play, which I had with me, and turned to Act II, Scene 2. "Here," I said, "you will see where Lady Macbeth says, 'I laid their daggers ready. He could not miss 'em. Had he not resembled my father as he slept, I had done it.' Do you see?" "No," said the American woman, bluntly, "I don't." "But it's simple!" I exclaimed. "I wonder I didn't see it years ago. The reason Duncan resembled Lady Macbeth's father as he slept is that *it actually was her father!*" "Good God!" breathed my companion, softly. "Lady Macbeth's father killed the King," I said, "and, hearing someone coming, thrust the body under the bed and crawled into the bed himself." "But," said the lady, "you can't have a murderer who only appears in the story once. You can't have that." "I know that," I said, and I turned to Act II, Scene 4. "It says here, 'Enter Ross with an old Man.' Now, that old man is never identified and it is my contention he was old Mr. Macbeth, whose ambition it was to make his daughter Queen. There you have your motive." "But even then," cried the American lady, "he's still a minor character!" "Not," I said, gleefully, "when you realized that he was also *one of the weird sisters in disguise!*" "You mean one of the three witches?" "Precisely," I said. "Listen to this speech of the old man's. 'On Tuesday last, a falcon towering in her pride of place, was by a mousing owl hawk'd at and kill'd.' Who does that sound like?" "It sounds like the way the three witches talk," said my companion, reluctantly. "Precisely!" I said again. "Well," said the American woman, "maybe you're right, but—" "I'm sure I am," I said. "And do you know what I'm going to do now?" "No," she said. "What?" "Buy a copy of *Hamlet*, I said, "and solve *that!*" My companion's eyes brightened. "Then," she said, "you don't think Hamlet did it?" "I am," I said, "absolutely positive he didn't." "But who," she demanded, "do you suspect?" I looked at her cryptically. "Everybody," I said, and disappeared into a small grove of trees as silently as I had come.

A Glimpse
of the Flatpaws

I F THE PATIENT and devoted English bloodhound is a plain-clothesman, the German shepherd is a harness bull. Until six years ago, eight or more German shepherds trotted beats, each accompanied by a police officer, over in Brooklyn. The canine cops had all been presented to the Brooklyn Police Department by private citizens, but they gradually died off, or were retired, and finally no new ones appeared to take their place. They were highly proficient, perfectly trained dog cops, and they brought many a felon to justice. This squad of Brooklyn flatpaws contained one policewoman named Peggy, whose record was just as good as that of the males. I went over to Brooklyn years ago for *The New Yorker's* "Talk of the Town" and met one of the police dogs, Nero, who was four years old at the time. We didn't shake hands. He growled low when I took a step toward him. "These dogs don't regard any man as their friend," Nero's partner, Patrolman Michael Mulcare, told me. I went back and sat down, and Nero stopped growling, but he kept his eye on me. An active, handsome, glossy animal, he wore his full equipment: collar, leash, and large leather muzzle with a broad, hard end. "They knock guys down with that muzzle," said Mulcare, "if they try to get away."

Nero walked over and sniffed me. "Hello, doggie," I said politely. Nero growled again.

"Don't move," said Mulcare. I didn't move. Mulcare commanded the dog to lie down, and he did. Then he was led away. "You can move now," said his partner.

Each dog patrolled a night beat in Flatbush with his officer. The patrolmen stayed on the streets, but, at the command "Search," the dogs went down dark alleys, into areaways, and over fences into the lawns of private houses, sniffing around for intruders. If a dog found a man—whether burglar, householder, swain throwing pebbles at a nursemaid's window, or whomever—he stood bristling beside him, growling loudly and ominously till the patrolman came up. The dog never attacked unless the man ran—or pulled a gun. If he ran, the dog dashed between his legs and tripped him, or made a flying tackle at the small of his back and knocked him down. If he pulled a gun, the dog attacked even more viciously, knocking the man down, working up to his gun hand, and, with claws and muzzle, disarming him. Gunfire merely infuriated a trained German shepherd.

The dogs practiced each day, going up ladders, climbing walls, getting into windows. Now and then at Police Department graduations—and at the Westminster Show—they put on exhibitions. They had been awarded many prizes, which were kept at the Police Academy. Once a shepherd named Rex, investigating a house closed for the season, grew suspicious of an open window on the back porch and went in to look around. When his growls and snarls brought his human partner, Rex had cornered in an upstairs room two thieves who were only too glad to surrender to a less dangerous cop.

If Brooklyn had maintained its night patrol of police dogs, they could have broken up the gang of youthful murderers that recently infested its parks and shocked the world with their meaningless killings. But the German shepherds in America have gradually been retired from police duty since the war, and are now known mainly for their work as Seeing Eye dogs. England has got far ahead of us in the use of trained shepherds to keep down nocturnal crime in the parks of its large cities. Scotland Yard has a force of more than one hundred and fifty Alsatians, and as a result of this alert patrol there were only thirteen cases of purse snatching in London's Hyde Park in 1954. In 1946, when the night watch was begun, there were eight hundred and thirty cases of purse snatching in that park.

I saw the Scotland Yard dogs in training when I was in London last June. I called at the Yard one morning and was taken out to the headquarters of the dogs in a police Humber, accompanied by Chief Superintendent John Tickle, then in charge of the flatpaws, and Chief Inspector Morgan Davies, who was about to take his turn in supervising the activities of the Alsatians. These dogs are actually German shepherds under an alias. The breed developed a reputation for ferocity in Germany even before the First World War, and the name was changed in England to free the dog from its stigma of savagery. The police dogs of Germany were trained by the use of whips and spiked collars, which tended to make them hostile to all men. The London dogs, as well as those used in Liverpool, Manchester, and Birmingham, undergo a fourteen-weeks course of training during which only kindness and patience are practiced by the dogs' handlers.

Unlike the shepherds of Germany and of Brooklyn, the Alsatians wear no muzzles and they are brought up in the homes of their handlers, usually married men with children. This has made them, if not exactly affable, far less fierce than the dogs of Germany, and considerably more hospitable than the old Brooklyn squad. I found that I could move among the Alsatians without being threatened or even insulted. The thirty young dogs I watched going through their first two weeks of routine lessons kept up a constant clamor, each in its own individual tone of voice, but there was no deep growling. One dog addressed me in a low singsong, something between a bartender's snarl and the crooning of a baby. I think he was daring me to cut and run.

I was shown how the dogs go about finding a man hidden in a tree, climbing ladders and fences, and chasing and pulling to earth an "escaping criminal." Each of the dogs took its turn chasing the man who posed as the fugitive and dragging him to the ground by seizing his sleeve just above the wrist. During each of these acts, the other dogs kept up a continual whining, tugging at their leashes and begging for the signal "Get him!" This is the part of their work they like best, and they have brought down many a culprit who has tried to break away from the handlers.

The dogs have an excellent record for good behavior, on and off duty. Their work has become known far and wide; last year two London-trained Alsatians were added to the police force of Bermuda, and while I was at the training grounds, twenty miles from London, two officers from Lebanon were being schooled in the handling of shepherds. Superintendent Tickle told me, above the babel of the rookies, that the Alsatians were presented to Scotland Yard by private owners. Thirty per cent of the canine candidates for the police force turn out to be unequipped for the work, because of too much pugnacity, or too much gentleness, or a downright lack of interest in climbing things or chasing people. These dogs are returned to their former masters as a rule, but some of the more aggressive ones join the Army or the Air Corps, where they are used as watch dogs for military establishments and air fields. Such installations are secure against saboteurs or night prowlers of any kind when they are guarded by a trained German shepherd.

Labradors, which were originally used, gradually disappeared from the police department because of a curious and false belief that this breed is not aggressive enough to deter criminals. The very existence of the Alsatian patrol, on the other hand, because of the German shepherd's indelible reputation, acts as a preventive of crime in the parks of London, as it would in those of Brooklyn and other parts of New York City. Knowing this from his years of experience with the dogs, Superintendent Tickle wrote a letter to the Police Commissioner of New York, explaining the work of his Alsatians, but he had not received a reply after more than six months. Police officers from Germany, as well as almost every other European country, have travelled to Wickham in Kent, where the dogs are trained, to act as observers of this most famous of police-dog patrols, but New York has not yet sent any officer to Scotland Yard.

The training of a German shepherd requires as much dogmanship in its handler as the training of a bloodhound, and not every officer is fitted for the job. It may be, for all I know, that Brooklyn's postwar patrolmen turned out to lack the special knack required for working with a dog as a partner. The Brooklyn system of training was a modification of the German system, without its whips and spiked collars, and what Superintendent Tickle and his successor would like to impress upon modern police departments is the efficacy of educating the dogs in the Scotland Yard manner. The dog that lives in its handler's home is more adaptable to training than the one that sees its partner only when the night beat gets under way.

My day at Wickham began at eleven o'clock in the morning, with tea in Superintendent Tickle's office out there. I signed a handsome guest book, a gift to the Wickham Headquarters from Douglas Fairbanks, who had recently made a film called *Police Dog* with the co-operation of Scotland Yard and its Alsatians. The walls of the office were hung with photographs of some of the outstanding heroes of the dog patrol, including the only dog in the force that was ever shot at. British criminals rarely carry guns. This dog was nicked in the ear by one bullet, and three other shots went wild before he closed in on his assailant and brought him down. Even though the dogs wear no muzzles, they never mangle or maul their quarry, but simply hold him until their human partner arrives to take over. A Labrador called Big Ben, who has been with the patrol since it began, has a place of honor in the photograph gallery, since he has brought about one hundred and thirty-three arrests during his nine-year career. Big Ben has little use for Alsatians, and, to prove that his own breed is as tough as any, if not tougher, he is always willing to take on any two Alsatians at the same time, the best day they ever saw.

Superintendent Tickle (who has recently been promoted and reassigned) is not a bloodhound man, and I was astonished to discover that he regards bloodhounds as lacking in courage. Inspector Davies had nothing to say about this theory, but I expressed my opinion one day in the London *Daily Mail*. I tried to point out that the difference between the German shepherd and the bloodhound is purely one of temperament and aptitude, like the difference between the patrolman and the plainclothes detective. I admitted that the bloodhound cannot climb ladders or fences, that it has never been known to knock anybody down except by accident, and that it would no sooner climb through an open window, looking for intruders, burly or otherwise, than I would, or my poodle Christabel. This is a matter of discretion, not a proof of cowardice, and it has kept me alive for sixty years, Christabel for fifteen, and the bloodhound breed for close to a thousand years.

I have no doubt that Big Ben could outdo a trained bloodhound in every aspect of police work except one, the successful following of an old, cold trail. The nose of the German shepherd, like that of the Labrador, has its limitations, and it must invariably give up on ancient trails that a bloodhound could take in his stride. In 1951, the Bloodhound Association of England challenged the Alsatians to a field trial, and the bloodhounds came out on top, but it was not a conclusive test because a lot of things went wrong, including some of the dogs on both sides, and their handlers. There are only two bloodhound trainers left in England who were training dogs before the war, most of the other trainers having been killed in action or grown too old for this highly specialized work. The little group of devoted private owners and breeders of bloodhounds in England goes doggedly on, however, holding a field trial every year, occasionally lending its hounds to the police of a city or town here and there in the British Isles.

The great English bloodhound, in his native land, has not kept up with his American brother, but he is still on his feet, and still willing and eager to take on police-trained Alsatians over a trail from twenty-four hours to two weeks old, or even colder than that. Perhaps some day there may be an annual international field trial in which the best German shepherds and bloodhounds of the United States and Great Britain take part. I shall be glad to present a Thurber Cup to be awarded each year at this competition. And may the best bloodhound win.

Tom, the Young Kidnapper, or, Pay Up and Live

(A kind of Horatio Alger story based on the successful $30,000 kidnapping in Kansas City of Miss Mary McElroy, who had a lovely time, whose abductors gave her roses and wept when she left, and whose father said he did not want the young men to go to the penitentiary)

I WOULD ADMIRE to walk with youse to a small dark cellar and manacle you to a damp wall."

The speaker was a young American, of perhaps twenty-five years, with a frank, open countenance. Betty Spencer, daughter of old Joab Spencer, the irate banker and the richest man in town, flushed prettily. Her would-be abductor flushed too, and stood twisting his hat in his hands. He was neatly, if flashily, dressed.

"I am sorry," she said, in a voice that was sweet and low, an excellent thing in woman, "I am sorry, but I am on my way to church, for my faith is as that of a little child."

"But I must have sixty or a hundred thousand dollars from your irate father tonight—or tomorrow at the latest," said Tom McGirt, for it was he. "It is not so much for me as for the 'gang.'"

"Do you belong to a gang?" cried Betty, flushing prettily, a look of admiration in her eyes. In his adoring embarrassment, the young kidnapper tore his hat into five pieces and ate them.

"My, but you must have a strong stomach!" cried the young lady.

"That was nothing," Tom said modestly. "Anybody would of done the same thing. You know what I wisht? I wisht it had been me stopping a horse that was running away with you at the risk of my life instead of eating a hat." He looked so forlorn and unhappy because no horse was running away with her that she pitied him.

"Does your gang really need the money?" she cried. "For if it really does, I should be proud to have you kidnap me and subject me to a most humiliating but broadening experience."

"The gang don't work, see?" said the young man, haltingly, for he hated to make this confession. "They're too young and strong to work—I mean there is so much to see and do and drink, and if they was working in a factory, say, or an old stuffy office all day, why—" She began to cry, tears welling up in her eyes.

"I shall come with you," she said, "for I believe that young men should be given hundreds of thousands of dollars that they may enjoy life. I wear a five-and-a-half glove, so I hope your manacles fit me, else I could easily escape from those which were too large."

"If we ain't got your size," he said, earnestly, drawing himself up to his full height, "I'll go through smoke and flame to git some for you. Because I—well, you see, I—"

"Yes?" she encouraged him, gently.

"Aw, I won't tell youse now," he said. "Some day when I have made myself worthy, I'll tell youse."

"I have faith in you," she said softly. "I know you will pull this job off. You can do it, and you *will* do it."

"Thanks, Betty," he said. "I appreciate your interest in me. You shall be proud some day of Tom the Young Kidnapper, or Pay Up and Live." He spoke the subtitle proudly.

"I'll go with you," she said. "No matter where."

"It ain't much of a basement," he said, reddening, and twisting an automatic between his fingers. "It's dark and the walls are damp, but me old mother ain't there, and that's something. She's no good," he added.

"I know," she said softly. They walked on slowly down the street to a nasty part of town where an automobile drew up alongside the curb, and they got in. Four young men with frank, open countenances were inside, their faces freshly scrubbed, their dark hair moistened and slicked down. Tom introduced them all, and they put away their automatics, and took off their hats, and grinned and were very polite. "I am quite happy," Betty told them.

The cellar in which the young gang manacled Betty to a wall was, as Tom promised, dark and damp, but the chains which fitted around her wrists were very nice and new and quite snug, so she was quite content. Two of the boys played tiddlywinks with her, while the others went out to mail a letter which she had written at the gang's dictation. It read: "Dear Father—Put a hundred thousand berries in an old tin box and drop it out of your car when you see a red light on the old Post Road tonight, or your daughter will never come home. If you tell the police we will bite her ears off."

"That's nice," said Betty, reading it over, "for it will afford Father an opportunity, now that I am in mortal danger, to realize how much he loves me and of how little worth money is, and it will show him also that the young men of this town are out to win!"

Betty was kept in the cellar all night, but in the morning Tom brought her chocolate and marmalade on an ivory-colored breakfast tray, and also a copy of Keats' poems, and a fluffy little kitten with a pink ribbon tied around its neck. One of the other boys brought her a table badminton set, and a third, named Thad the Slasher, or Knife Them and Run, brought her a swell Welsh pony named Rowdy.

"Oh," said Betty, "I am so happy I could cry," and she jangled her manacles. Several of the boys did cry, she looked so uncomfortable and so happy, and then Betty cried, and then they all laughed, and put a record on the Victrola.

That night, Betty was still chained to the wall because her father had not "come through." "He's holding out for only forty grand," explained Tom, reluctantly, for he did not wish her to know that her father was stingy. "I don't guess your father realizes that we really will make away with you if he don't kick in. He thinks mebbe it's a bluff, but we mean business!" His eyes flashed darkly, and Betty's eyes snapped brightly.

"I know you do!" she cried. "Why, it's been worth forty thousand just the experience I've had. I *do* hope he gives you the hundred thousand, for I should like to go back alive and tell everybody how sweet you have been and how lovely it is to be kidnapped!"

On the second morning, Betty was sitting on the damp cellar floor playing Guess Where I Am with Tom and Ned and Dick and Sluggy, when Thad came in, toying with his frank, open clasp knife, his genial countenance clouded by a frown.

"What is wrong, Thad," asked Betty, "for I perceive that something is wrong?" Thad stood silent, kicking the moist dirt of the floor with the toe of his shoe. He rubbed a sleeve against his eye.

"The old man has come through with the dough," he said. "We—we gotta let you go now." He began to cry openly. Tom paled. One of the boys took Betty's chains off. Betty gathered up her presents, the kitty, and the table badminton kit, and the poems. "Rowdy is saddled an' waitin' outside," said Thad, brokenly, handing tens and twenties, one at a time, to his pals.

"Goodbyeee," cried Betty. She turned to Tom. "Goodbyeee, Tom," she said.

"Goo—" said Tom, and stopped, all choked up.

When Betty arrived at her house, it was full of policemen and relatives. She dropped her presents and ran up to her father, kindly old Judge Spencer, for he had become a kindly old judge while she was in the cellar, and was no longer the irate old banker and no longer, indeed, the town's richest man, for he only had about seven hundred dollars left.

"My child!" he cried. "I wish to reward these young men for teaching us all a lesson. I have become a poorer but less irate man, and even Chief of Police Jackson here has profited by this abduction, for he has been unable to apprehend the culprits and it has taken some of the cockiness out of him, I'll be bound."

"That is true, Joab," said the Chief of Police, wiping away a tear. "Those young fellows have shown us all the errors of our ways."

"Have they skipped out, Betty?" asked her father.

"Yes, Father," said Betty and a tear welled up into her eye.

"Ha, ha!" said old Judge Spencer. "I'll wager there was one young man whom you liked better than the rest, eh, my chick? Well, I should like to give him a position and invite him to Sunday dinner. His rescuing you from the flames of that burning shack for only a hundred thous—"

"I didn't do *that*, sir" said a modest voice, and they all turned and looked at the speaker, Tom the Kidnapper, for it was he. "I simply let her loose from the cellar, after we got the dough."

"It's the same thing," said her father, with mock sternness. "Young man, we have been watching you these past two days— that is to say, we have been wondering where you were. You have outwitted us all and been charming to my daughter. You deserve your fondest wish. What will you have?"

"I'll have Scotch-and-soda, sir," said Tom. "And your daughter's hand."

"Ha, ha!" said the kindly old judge. "There's enterprise for you, Jenkins!" He nudged Jenkins in the ribs and the Chief nudged back, and laughed. So they all had a Scotch-and-soda and then the Judge married his blushing daughter, right then and there, to Tom the Young Kidnapper, or If You Yell We'll Cut Your Throat.

Two Dogs

ONE SULTRY MOONLESS NIGHT, a leopard escaped from a circus and slunk away into the shadows of a city. The chief of police dogs assigned to the case a German shepherd named Plunger and a plainclothes bloodhound named Plod. Plod was a slow, methodical sleuth, but his uniformed partner was restless and impatient. Plod set the pace until Plunger snapped, "We couldn't catch a turtle this way," and bounded along the trail like a whippet. He got lost. When Plod found him, half an hour later, the bloodhound said, "It is better to get somewhere slowly than nowhere fast."

"Repose is for the buried," said the police dog. "I even chase cats in my dreams."

"I don't," said the bloodhound. "Out of scent, out of mind."

As they went along, each in his own way, through the moonlessness, they exchanged further observations on life.

"He who hunts and turns away may live to hunt another day," commented Plod.

"*Runs* away, you mean," sneered Plunger.

"I never run," said the bloodhound. "It's no good trailing a cat when you're out of breath, especially if the cat isn't. I figured that out myself. They call it instinct."

"I was taught to do what I do, and not to do what I don't," the police dog said. "They call it discipline. When *I* catch cats, cats stay caught," he added.

"I don't catch them, I merely find out where they are," the bloodhound said quietly.

The two dogs suddenly made out a great dark house looming in front of them at the end of a lane. "The trail ends right here, twenty feet from that window," the bloodhound said, sniffing a certain spot. "The leopard must have leaped into the house from here."

The two dogs stared into the open window of the dark and silent house.

"I was taught to jump through the open windows of dark houses," said Plunger.

"I taught myself not to," said Plod. "I wouldn't grab that cat if I were you. I never grab a leopard unless it is a coat." But Plunger wasn't listening.

"Here goes," he said jauntily, and he jumped through the window of the dark and silent house. Instantly there was a racket that sounded to the keen ears of the bloodhound like a police dog being forcibly dressed in women's clothes by a leopard, and that is precisely what it was. All of a moment, Plunger, dressed in women's clothes from hat to shoes, with a pink parasol thrust under his collar, came hurtling out the window. "I had my knee on his chest, too," said the bewildered police dog plaintively.

The old sleuth sighed. "He lasteth longest and liveth best who gets not his knee on his quarry's chest," murmured Plod, in cloudy English but fluent Bloodhound.

Moral: Who would avoid life's wriest laughter should not attain the thing he's after.

The Whip-Poor-Will

THE NIGHT HAD JUST BEGUN to get pale around the edges when the whip-poor-will began. Kinstrey, who slept in a back room on the first floor, facing the meadow and the strip of woods beyond, heard a blind man tapping and a bugle calling and a woman screaming "Help! Police!" The sergeant in grey was cutting open envelopes with a sword. "Sit down there, sit down there, sit down there!" he chanted at Kinstrey. "Sit down there, cut your throat, cut your throat, whip-poor-will, whip-poor-will, whip-poor-will!" And Kinstrey woke up.

He opened his eyes, but lay without moving for several minutes, separating the fantastic morning from the sounds and symbols of his dream. There was the palest wash of light in the room. Kinstrey scowled through tousled hair at his wristwatch and saw that it was ten minutes past four. "Whip-poor-will, whip-poor-will, whip-poor-will!" The bird sounded very near—in the grass outside the window, perhaps. Kinstrey got up and went to the window in his bare feet and looked out. You couldn't tell where the thing was. The sound was all around you, incredibly loud and compelling and penetrating. Kinstrey had never heard a whip-poor-will so near at hand before. He had heard them as a boy in Ohio in the country, but he remembered their call as faint and plaintive and faraway, dying before long somewhere between

191

the hills and the horizon. You didn't hear the bird often in Ohio, it came back to him, and it almost never ventured as close to a house or barn as this brazen-breasted bird murdering sleep out there along the fence line somewhere. "Whip-poor-will, whip-poor-will, whip-poor-will!" Kinstrey climbed back into bed and began to count; the bird did twenty-seven whips without pausing. His lungs must be built like a pelican's pouch, or a puffin or a penguin or pemmican or a paladin. . . . It was bright daylight when Kinstrey fell asleep again.

At breakfast, Madge Kinstrey, looking cool and well rested in her white piqué house coat, poured the coffee with steady authority. She raised her eyebrows slightly in mild surprise when Kinstrey mentioned the whip-poor-will the second time (she had not listened the first time, for she was lost in exploring with a long, sensitive finger an infinitesimal chip on the rim of her coffee cup).

"Whip-poor-will?" she said, finally. "No, I didn't hear it. Of course, my room is on the front of the house. You must have been slept out and ready to wake up anyway, or you wouldn't have heard it."

"Ready to wake up?" said Kinstrey. "At four o'clock in the morning? I hadn't slept three hours."

"Well, I didn't hear it," said Mrs. Kinstrey. "I don't listen for night noises; I don't even hear the crickets or the frogs."

"Neither do I," said Kinstrey. "It's not the same thing. This thing is loud as a fire bell. You can hear it for a mile."

"I didn't hear it," she said, buttering a piece of thin toast.

Kinstrey gave it up and turned his scowling attention to the headlines in the *Herald Tribune* of the day before. The vision of his wife sleeping quietly in her canopied four-poster came between his eyes and the ominous headlines. Madge always slept quietly, almost without moving, her arms straight and still outside the covers, her fingers relaxed. She did not believe anyone had to toss and turn. "It's a notion," she would tell Kinstrey. "Don't let your nerves get the best of you. Use your will power."

"Um, hm," said Kinstrey aloud, not meaning to.

"Yes, sir?" said Arthur, the Kinstrey's colored butler, offering Kinstrey a plate of hot blueberry muffins.

"Nothing," said Kinstrey, looking at his wife. "Did you hear the whip-poor-will, Arthur?"

"No, sir, I didn't," said Arthur.

"Did Margaret?"

"I don't think she did, sir," said Arthur. "She didn't say anything about it."

The next morning the whip-poor-will began again at the same hour, rolling out its loops and circles of sound across the new day. Kinstrey, in his dreams, was beset by trios of little bearded men rolling hoops at him. He tried to climb up onto a gigantic Ferris wheel whose swinging seats were rumpled beds. The round cop with wheels for feet rolled toward him shouting, "Will power will, will power will, whip-poor-will!"

Kinstrey opened his eyes and stared at the ceiling and began to count the whips. At one point the bird did fifty-three straight, without pausing. I suppose, like the drops of water or the bright light in the third degree, this could drive you nuts, Kinstrey thought. Or make you confess. He began to think of things he hadn't thought of for years: the time he took the quarter from his mother's pocketbook, the time he steamed open a letter addressed to his father; it was from his teacher in the eighth grade. Miss—let's see—Miss Willpool, Miss Whippoor, Miss Will Power, Miss Wilmott—that was it.

He had reached the indiscretions of his middle twenties when the whip-poor-will suddenly stopped, on "poor," not on "will." Something must have frightened it. Kinstrey sat up on the edge of the bed and lighted a cigarette and listened. The bird was through calling all right, but Kinstrey couldn't go back to sleep. The day was bright as a flag. He got up and dressed.

"I thought you weren't going to smoke cigarettes before breakfast anymore," said Madge later. "I found four stubs in the ashtray in your bedroom."

It was no use telling her he had smoked them before going to bed; you couldn't fool Madge; she always knew. "That goddamn bird woke me up again," he said, "and this time I couldn't get back to sleep." He passed her his empty coffee cup. "It did fifty-three without stopping this morning," he added. "I don't know how the hell it breathes."

His wife took his coffee cup and set it down firmly. "Not three cups," she said. "Not with you sleeping so restlessly the way it is."

"You didn't hear it, I suppose?" he said.

She poured herself some more coffee. "No," she said, "I didn't hear it."

Margaret hadn't heard it, either, but Arthur had. Kinstrey talked to them in the kitchen while they were clearing up after breakfast. Arthur said that it "wuk" him but he went right back to sleep. He said he slept like a log—must be the air off the ocean. As for Margaret, she always slept like a log; only thing ever kept her awake was people a-hoopin' and a-hollerin'. She was glad she didn't hear the whip-poor-will. Down where she came from, she said, if you heard a whip-poor-will singing near the house, it meant there was going to be a death. Arthur said he had heard about that, too; must have been his grandma told him, or somebody.

If a whip-poor-will singing near the house meant death, Kinstrey told them, it wouldn't really make any difference whether you heard it or not. "It doesn't make any difference whether you see the ladder you're walking under," he said, lighting a cigarette and watching the effect of his words on Margaret. She turned from putting some plates away, and her eyes widened and rolled a little.

"Mr. Kinstrey is just teasin' you, Mag," said Arthur, who smiled and was not afraid. Thinks he's pretty smart, Kinstrey thought. Just a little bit too smart, maybe. Kinstrey remembered Arthur's way of smiling, almost imperceptibly, at things Mrs. Kinstrey sometimes said to her husband when Arthur was just coming into the room or just going out—little things that were none of his business to listen to. Like "Not three cups of coffee if a bird keeps you awake." Wasn't that what she had said?

"Is there any more coffee?" he asked, testily. "Or did you throw it out?" He knew they had thrown it out; breakfast had been over for almost an hour.

"We can make you some fresh," said Arthur.

"Never mind," said Kinstrey. "Just don't be so sure of yourself. There's nothing in life to be sure about."

When, later in the morning, he started out the gate to walk down to the post office, Madge called to him from an upstairs window. "Where are you going?" she asked, amiably enough. He frowned up at her. "To the taxidermist's," he said, and went on.

He realized, as he walked along in the warm sunlight, that he had made something of a spectacle of himself. Just because he hadn't had enough sleep—or enough coffee. It wasn't his fault, though. It was that infernal bird. He discovered, after a quarter of a mile, that the imperative rhythm of the whip-poor-will's call was running through his mind, but the words of the song were new: fatal bell, fatal bell, fa-tal bell. Now, where had that popped up from? It took him some time to place it; it was a fragment from *Macbeth*. There was something about the fatal bellman crying in the night. "The fatal bellman cried the livelong night"— something like that. It was an owl that cried the night Duncan was murdered. Funny thing to call up after all these years; he hadn't read the play since college. It was that fool Margaret, talking about the whip-poor-will and the old superstition that if you hear the whip-poor-will singing near the house, it means there is going to be a death. Here it was 1942, and people still believed in stuff like that.

The next day the dream induced by the calling of the whip-poor-will was longer and more tortured—a nightmare filled with dark perils and heavy hopelessness. Kinstrey woke up trying to cry out. He lay there breathing hard and listening to the bird. He began to count: one, two, three, four, five . . .

Then, suddenly, he leaped out of bed and ran to the window

and began yelling and pounding on the windowpane and running the blind up and down. He shouted and cursed until his voice got hoarse. The bird kept right on going. He slammed the window down and turned away from it, and there was Arthur in the doorway.

"What is it, Mr. Kinstrey?" said Arthur. He was fumbling with the end of a faded old bathrobe and trying to blink the sleep out of his eyes. "Is anything the matter?"

Kinstrey glared at him. "Get out of here!" he shouted. "And put some coffee on. Or get me a brandy or something."

"I'll put some coffee on," said Arthur. He went shuffling away in his slippers, still half asleep.

"Well," said Madge Kinstrey over her coffee cup at breakfast. "I hope you got your tantrum over and done with this morning. I never heard such a spectacle—squalling like a spoiled brat."

"You can't hear spectacles," said Kinstrey, coldly. "You see them."

"I'm sure I don't know what you're talking about," she said.

No, you don't, thought Kinstrey, you never have; never have, nev-er have, nev-er have. Would he get that damned rhythm out of his head? It struck him that perhaps Madge had no subconscious. When she lay on her back, her eyes closed; when she got up, they opened, like a doll's. The mechanism of her mind was as simple as a cigarette box; it was either open or it was closed, and there was nothing else, nothing else . . .

The whole problem turns on a very neat point, Kinstrey thought as he lay awake that night, drumming on the headboard with his fingers. William James would have been interested in it; Henry, too, probably. I've got to ignore this thing, get adjusted to it, become oblivious of it. I mustn't fight it, I mustn't build it up. If I get to screaming at it, I'll be running across that wet grass out there in my bare feet, charging that bird as if it were a trench full of Germans, throwing rocks at it, giving the Rebel yell or something, for God's sake. No, I mustn't build it up. I'll think of something else every time it pops into my mind. I'll name the

Dodger infield to myself, over and over: Camilli, Herman, Reese, Vaughan, Camilli, Herman, Reese . . .

Kinstrey did not succeed in becoming oblivious of the whip-poor-will. Its dawn call pecked away at his dreams like a vulture at a heart. It slowly carved out a recurring nightmare in which Kinstrey was attacked by an umbrella whose handle, when you clutched it, clutched right back, for the umbrella was not an umbrella at all but a raven. Through the gloomy hallways of his mind rang the Thing's dolorous cry: nevermore, nevermore, nevermore, whip-poor-will, whip-poor-will . . .

One day, Kinstrey asked Mr. Tetford at the post office if the whip-poor-wills ever went away. Mr. Tetford squinted at him. "Don't look like the sun was brownin' you up none," he said. "I don't know as they ever go away. They move around. I like to hear 'em. You get used to 'em."

"Sure," said Kinstrey. "What do people do when they can't get used to them, though—I mean old ladies or sick people?"

"Only one's been bothered was old Miss Purdy. She darn near set fire to the whole island tryin' to burn 'em out of her woods. Shootin' at 'em might drive 'em off, or a body could trap 'em easy enough and let 'em loose somewheres else. But people get used to 'em after a few mornings."

"Oh, sure," said Kinstrey. "Sure."

That evening in the living room, when Arthur brought in the coffee, Kinstrey's cup cackled idiotically in its saucer when he took it off the tray.

Madge Kinstrey laughed. "Your hand is shaking like a leaf," she said.

He drank all his coffee at once and looked up savagely. "If I could get one good night's sleep, it might help," he said. "That damn bird! I'd like to wring its neck."

"Oh, come, now," she said, mockingly. "You wouldn't hurt a fly. Remember the mouse we caught in the Westport house? You took it out in the field and let it go."

"The trouble with you—" he began, and stopped. He opened

the lid of a cigarette box and shut it, opened and shut it again, reflectively. "As simple as that," he said.

She dropped her amused smile and spoke shortly. "You're acting like a child about that silly bird," she said. "Worse than a child. I was over at the Barrys' this afternoon. Even their little Ann didn't make such a fuss. A whip-poor-will frightened her the first morning, but now she never notices them."

"I'm not frightened, for God's sake!" shouted Kinstrey. "Frightened or brave, asleep or awake, open or shut—you make everything black or white."

"Well," she said, "I like that."

"I think the bird wakes you up, too," he said. "I think it wakes up Arthur and Margaret."

"And we just pretend it doesn't?" she asked. "Why on earth should we?"

"Oh, out of some fool notion of superiority, I suppose. Out of—I don't know."

"I'll thank you not to class me with the servants," she said coldly. He lighted a cigarette and didn't say anything. "You're being ridiculous and childish," she said, "fussing about nothing at all, like an invalid in a wheelchair." She got up and started from the room.

"Nothing at all," he said, watching her go.

She turned at the door. "Ted Barry says he'll take you on at tennis if your bird hasn't worn you down too much." She went on up the stairs, and he heard her close the door of her room.

He sat smoking moodily for a long time, and fell to wondering whether the man's wife in "The Raven" had seen what the man had seen perched on the pallid bust of Pallas just above the chamber door. Probably not, he decided. When he went to bed, he lay awake a long while trying to think of the last line of "The Raven." He couldn't get any further than "Like a demon that is dreaming," and this kept running through his head. "Nuts," he said at last, aloud, and he had the oddly disturbing feeling it wasn't he who had spoken but somebody else.

* * *

Kinstrey was not surprised that Madge was a little girl in pigtails and a play suit. The long grey hospital room was filled with poor men in will chairs, running their long, sensitive fingers around the rims of empty coffee cups. "Poor Will, poor Will," chanted Madge, pointing her finger at him. "Here are your spectacles, here are your spectacles." One of the sick men was Arthur, grinning at him, grinning at him and holding him with one hand, so that he was powerless to move his arms and legs. "Hurt a fly, hurt a fly," chanted Madge. "Whip him now, whip him now!" she cried, and she was the umpoor in the high chair beside the court, holding a black umbrella over her head; love thirty, love forty, forty-one, forty-two, forty-three, forty-four. His feet were stuck in the wet concrete on his side of the net and Margaret peered over the net at him, holding a skillet for a racquet. Arthur was pushing him down now, and he was caught in the concrete from head to foot. It was Madge laughing and counting over him: refer-three, refer-four, refer-five, refer-will, repoor-will, whip-poor-will, whip-poor-will, whip-poor-will . . .

The dream still clung to Kinstrey's mind like a cobweb as he stood in the kitchen in his pyjamas and bare feet, wondering what he wanted, what he was looking for. He turned on the cold water in the sink and filled a glass, but only took a sip, and put it down. He left the water running. He opened the breadbox and took out half a loaf wrapped in oiled paper, and pulled open a drawer. He took out the bread knife and then put it back and took out the long, sharp carving knife. He was standing there holding the knife in one hand and the bread in the other when the door to the dining room opened. It was Arthur. "Who do you do first?" Kinstrey said to him, hoarsely. . . .

The Barrys, on their way to the beach in their station wagon, drove into the driveway between the house and the barn. They were surprised to see that, at a quarter to eleven in the morning, the Kinstrey servants hadn't taken in the milk. The bottle, standing on the small back porch, was hot to Barry's touch. When he couldn't rouse anyone, pounding and calling, he climbed up on the cellar door and looked in the kitchen window. He told his wife sharply to get back in the car. . . .

The local police and the state troopers were in and out of the house all day. It wasn't every morning of the year that you got called out on a triple murder and suicide.

It was just getting dark when Troopers Baird and Lennon came out of the front door and walked down to their car, pulled up beside the road in front of the house. Out in back, probably in the little strip of wood there, Lennon figured, a whip-poor-will began to call. Lennon listened a minute. "You ever hear the old people say a whip-poor-will singing near a house means death?" he asked.

Baird grunted and got in under the wheel. Lennon climbed in beside him. "Take more'n a whip-poor-will to cause a mess like that," said Trooper Baird, starting the car.

Destinations.

The Lady on 142

THE TRAIN was twenty minutes late, we found out when we bought our tickets, so we sat down on a bench in the little waiting room of the Cornwall Bridge station. It was too hot outside in the sun. This midsummer Saturday had got off to a sulky start, and now, at three in the afternoon, it sat, sticky and restive, in our laps.

There were several others besides Sylvia and myself waiting for the train to get in from Pittsfield: a colored woman who fanned herself with a *Daily News,* a young lady in her twenties reading a book, a slender, tanned man sucking dreamily on the stem of an unlighted pipe. In the center of the room, leaning against a high iron radiator, a small girl stared at each of us in turn, her mouth open, as if she had never seen people before. The place had the familiar, pleasant smell of railroad stations in the country, of something compounded of wood and leather and smoke. In the cramped space behind the ticket window, a telegraph instrument clicked intermittently, and once or twice a phone rang and the stationmaster answered it briefly. I couldn't hear what he said.

I was glad, on such a day, that we were going only as far as Gaylordsville, the third stop down the line, twenty-two minutes away. The stationmaster had told us that our tickets were the first tickets to Gaylordsville he had ever sold. I was idly pondering this small distinction when a train whistle blew in the distance. We all got to our feet, but the stationmaster came out of his cubbyhole and told us it was not our train but the 12:45 from New York, northbound. Presently the train thundered in like a hurricane and sighed ponderously to a stop. The stationmaster went out onto the platform and came back after a minute or two. The train got heavily under way again, for Canaan.

I was opening a pack of cigarettes when I heard the stationmaster talking on the phone again. This time his words came out clearly. He kept repeating one sentence. He was saying, "Conductor Reagan on 142 has the lady the office was asking about." The person on the other end of the line did not appear to get the meaning of the sentence. The stationmaster repeated it and hung up. For some reason, I figured that he did not understand it either.

Sylvia's eyes had the lost, reflective look they wear when she is trying to remember in what box she packed the Christmas-tree ornaments. The expressions on the faces of the colored woman, the young lady, and the man with the pipe had not changed. The little staring girl had gone away.

Our train was not due for another five minutes, and I sat back and began trying to reconstruct the lady on 142, the lady Conductor Reagan had, the lady the office was asking about. I moved nearer to Sylvia and whispered, "See if the trains are numbered in your timetable." She got the timetable out of her handbag and looked at it. "One forty-two," she said, "is the 12:45 from New York." This was the train that had gone by a few minutes before. "The woman was taken sick," said Sylvia. "They are probably arranging to have a doctor or her family meet her."

The colored woman looked around at her briefly. The young woman, who had been chewing gum, stopped chewing. The man with the pipe seemed oblivious. I lighted a cigarette and sat thinking. "The woman on 142," I said to Sylvia, finally, "might be almost anything, but she definitely is not sick." The only person who did not stare at me was the man with the pipe. Sylvia gave me her temperature-taking look, a cross between anxiety and vexation. Just then our train whistled and we all stood up. I picked up our two bags and Sylvia took the sack of string beans we had picked for the Connells.

When the train came clanking in, I said in Sylvia's ear, "He'll sit near us. You watch." "Who? Who will?" she said. "The stranger," I told her, "the man with the pipe."

Sylvia laughed. "He's not a stranger," she said. "He works for the Breeds." I was certain that he didn't. Women like to place people; every stranger reminds them of somebody.

The man with the pipe was sitting three seats in front of us, across the aisle, when we got settled. I indicated him with a nod of my head. Sylvia took a book out of the top of her overnight bag and opened it. "What's the matter with you?" she demanded. I looked around before replying. A sleepy man and woman sat across from us. Two middle-aged women in the seat in front of us were discussing the severe griping pain one of them had experienced as the result of an inflamed diverticulum. A slim, dark-eyed young woman sat in the seat behind us. She was alone.

"The trouble with women," I began, "is that they explain everything by illness. I have a theory that we would be celebrating the twelfth of May or even the sixteenth of April as Independence Day if Mrs. Jefferson hadn't got the idea her husband had a fever and put him to bed."

Sylvia found her place in the book. "We've been all through that before," she said. "Why couldn't the woman on 142 be sick?"

That was easy. I told her. "Conductor Reagan," I said, "got off the train at Cornwall Bridge and spoke to the stationmaster. 'I've got the woman the office was asking about,' he said."

Sylvia cut in. "He said 'lady.'"

I gave the little laugh that annoys her. "All conductors say 'lady,'" I explained. "Now, if a woman had got sick on the train, Reagan would have said, 'A woman got sick on my train. Tell the office.' What must have happened is that Reagan found, somewhere between Kent and Cornwall Bridge, a woman the office had been looking for."

Sylvia didn't close her book, but she looked up. "Maybe she got sick before she got on the train, and the office was worried," said Sylvia. She was not giving the problem close attention.

"If the office knew she got on the train," I said patiently, "they wouldn't have asked Reagan to let them know if he found her. They would have told him about her when she got on." Sylvia resumed her reading.

"Let's stay out of it," she said. "It isn't any of our business."

I hunted for my Chiclets but couldn't find them. "It might be everybody's business," I said, "every patriot's."

"I know, I know," said Sylvia. "You think she's a spy. Well, I still think she's sick."

I ignored that. "Every conductor on the line has been asked to look out for her," I said. "Reagan found her. She won't be met by her family. She'll be met by the FBI."

"Or the OPA," said Sylvia. "Alfred Hitchcock things don't happen on the New York, New Haven & Hartford."

I saw the conductor coming from the other end of the coach. "I'm going to tell the conductor," I said, "that Reagan on 142 has got the woman."

"No, you're not," said Sylvia. "You're not going to get us mixed up in this. He probably knows anyway."

The conductor, short, stocky, silvery-haired, and silent, took up our tickets. He looked like a kindly Ickes. Sylvia, who had stiffened, relaxed when I let him go by without a word about the woman on 142. "He looks exactly as if he knew where the Maltese Falcon is hidden, doesn't he?" said Sylvia, with the laugh that annoys me.

"Nevertheless," I pointed out, "you said a little while ago that he probably knows about the woman on 142. If she's just sick, why should they tell the conductor on *this* train? I'll rest more easily when I know that they've actually got her."

Sylvia kept on reading as if she hadn't heard me. I leaned my head against the back of the seat and closed my eyes.

The train was slowing down noisily and a brakeman was yelling "Kent! Kent!" when I felt a small, cold pressure against my shoulder. "Oh," the voice of the woman in the seat behind me said, "I've dropped my copy of *Coronet* under your seat." She leaned closer and her voice became low and hard. "Get off here, Mister," she said.

"We're going to Gaylordsville," I said.

"You and your wife are getting off here, Mister," she said.

I reached for the suitcases on the rack. "What do you want, for heaven's sake?" asked Sylvia.

"We're getting off here," I told her.

"Are you *really* crazy?" she demanded. "This is only Kent."

"Come on, sister," said the woman's voice. "You take the overnight bag and the beans. You take the big bag, Mister."

Sylvia was furious. "I *knew* you'd get us into this," she said to me, "shouting about spies at the top of your voice."

That made me angry. "You're the one that mentioned spies," I told her. "I didn't."

"You kept talking about it and talking about it," said Sylvia.

"Come on, get off, the two of you," said the cold, hard voice.

We got off. As I helped Sylvia down the steps, I said, "We know too much."

"Oh, shut up," she said.

We didn't have far to go. A big black limousine waited a few steps away. Behind the wheel sat a heavy-set foreigner with cruel lips and small eyes. He scowled when he saw us. "The boss don't want nobody up deh," he said.

"It's all right, Karl," said the woman. "Get in," she told us. We climbed into the back seat. She sat between us, with the gun in her hand. It was a handsome jeweled derringer.

"Alice will be waiting for us at Gaylordsville," said Sylvia, "in all this heat."

The house was a long, low, rambling building, reached at the end of a poplar-lined drive. "Never mind the bags," said the woman. Sylvia took the string beans and her book and we got out. Two huge mastiffs came bounding off the terrace, snarling. "Down, Mata!" said the woman. "Down, Pedro!" They slunk away, still snarling.

Sylvia and I sat side by side on a sofa in a large, handsomely appointed living room. Across from us, in a chair, lounged a tall man with heavily lidded black eyes and long, sensitive fingers. Against the door through which we had entered the room leaned a thin, undersized young man, with his hands in the pockets of his coat and a cigarette hanging from his lower lip. He had a drawn, sallow face and his small, half-closed eyes stared at us incuriously. In a corner of the room, a squat, swarthy man twiddled with the dials of a radio. The woman paced up and down, smoking a cigarette in a long holder.

"Well, Gail," said the lounging man in a soft voice, "to what do we owe thees unexpected visit?"

Gail kept pacing. "They got Sandra," she said finally.

The lounging man did not change expression. "Who got Sandra, Gail?" he asked softly.

"Reagan, on 142," said Gail.

The squat, swarthy man jumped to his feet. "All da time Egypt say keel dees Reagan!" he shouted. "All da time Egypt say bomp off dees Reagan!"

The lounging man did not look at him. "Sit down, Egypt," he said quietly. The swarthy man sat down. Gail went on talking.

"The punk here shot off his mouth," she said. "He was wise." I looked at the man leaning against the door.

"She means you," said Sylvia, and laughed.

"The dame was dumb," Gail went on. "She thought the lady on the train was sick."

I laughed. "She means you," I said to Sylvia.

"The punk was blowing his top all over the train," said Gail. "I had to bring 'em along."

Sylvia, who had the beans on her lap, began breaking and stringing them. "Well, my dear lady," said the lounging man, "a mos' homely leetle tawtch."

"Wozza totch?" demanded Egypt.

"Touch," I told him.

Gail sat down in a chair. "Who's going to rub 'em out?" she asked.

"Freddy," said the lounging man. Egypt was on his feet again.

"Na! Na!" he shouted. "Na da ponk! Da ponk bomp off da las' seex, seven peop'!"

The lounging man looked at him. Egypt paled and sat down.

"I thought *you* were the punk," said Sylvia. I looked at her coldly.

"I know where I have seen you before," I said to the lounging man. "It was at Zagreb, in 1927. Tilden took you in straight sets, six-love, six-love, six-love."

The man's eyes glittered. "I theenk I bomp off thees man myself," he said.

Freddy walked over and handed the lounging man an automatic. At this moment, the door Freddy had been leaning against burst open and in rushed the man with the pipe, shouting, "Gail! Gail! Gail! . . ."

"Gaylordsville! Gaylordsville!" bawled the brakeman. Sylvia was shaking me by the arm. "Quit moaning," she said. "Everybody is looking at you." I rubbed my forehead with a handkerchief. "Hurry up!" said Sylvia. "They don't stop here long." I pulled the bags down and we got off.

"Have you got the beans?" I asked Sylvia.

Alice Connell was waiting for us. On the way to their home in the car, Sylvia began to tell Alice about the woman on 142. I didn't say anything.

"He thought she was a spy," said Sylvia.

They both laughed. "She probably got sick on the train," said Alice. "They were probably arranging for a doctor to meet her at the station."

"That's just what I told him," said Sylvia.

I lighted a cigarette. "The lady on 142," I said firmly, "was definitely not sick."

"Oh, Lord," said Sylvia, "here we go again."